REASONABLE DOUBT

by Steven Barish

To My Family

Min and Bernie
Ken and Bob
Harriet and Jenny
and
Rachel

I had no part in choosing any of you. What a lucky man I am.

Acknowledgements

The narrator of this book, and one other character, are deaf. I am not. I could not have written *Reasonable Doubt*, therefore, if it had not been for the experiences I've shared with my deaf friends and colleagues over the past nine years. *Reasonable Doubt* is not a roman à clef. There are no real people here under falsified names, but it was working, living, and playing with deaf people that gave me the knowledge and insights necessary to create believable deaf characters.

In addition, I was fortunate to find several deaf friends who were willing to serve as unpaid editors. Rich Pelletier, Steve Weiner, Tammy Weiner, Jan Gemmill, Michele Westfall, Laura Bergan, and Alisa Butler read the manuscript in progress and suffered not knowing "who" for many months. The manuscript is better for their input and constructive criticism. Any mistakes or inaccuracies remaining are my responsibility, not theirs.

I had other unpaid editors, two of whom I also need to thank here. Rich Manley and Cindy Rohr-Redding can hear but were equally helpful and also suffered through reading a murder mystery at the rate of a chapter a week, or slower. Somehow, all of the above are still friends of mine.

There are also several people who had no direct link to this book that I need to thank publicly. Their contributions were to me, as a person. Without their gifts I would not be the writer I am. Thank you:

> Joanne Haupt—for laughter and innocence just when I needed them the most.
>
> Vincent MacNeill—for giving me the bug and for, once upon a time, travelling from Milwaukee to San Francisco via New York.
>
> Chris Ahalt—for more than 17 years of one-on-one athletic competition and, more importantly, best friendship.
>
> Sherry Holland—for much, much more than I could ever write here. Maybe, now that this is in print, for all the world to see, you'll finally believe me.

Lastly, there is one person who belongs in both of the above categories. No one has been more important to this book than fellow writer, Kristin Keegan. She was my toughest and most astute critic. I started the book without her but shortly afterward she became my primary inspiration and support. She gave me the physical details of the murder scene, helped create the plot, and acted as my California research assistant. In the latter stages she provided the space for me to write and type. Her contributions to my growth as a person are equally as great.

S.B.

Laurel, Md.; Berkeley, Calif.
Jan.–Aug. 1983

1

I do not believe in God, but I do believe in faith. Since this is a story about murder, not theology, I will explain that sentence as briefly as possible. A fellow atheist once told me that faith was stupidity: belief without evidence.

No one has ever proven to me that God exists so I don't believe in him/her/it. Yet this is a story of my faith *against* the evidence. It starts with a call from Tom, telling me that he was in jail, accused of murder, caught with the equivalent of a smoking gun in his hand. The police described it as an open-and-shut case but Tom said he was innocent.

What I mean by faith is that at that very moment I *knew* he was innocent. It would not have mattered to me if a dozen witnesses had sworn on their bibles that they had seen him "pull the trigger" or whatever. I knew Tom and knew that he couldn't have killed anyone, much less Sarah. So, I packed a suitcase and took a taxi to the airport. I charged my ticket with plastic money, I was down to $100 and change in cash, and flew 3000 miles west to see what I could do to help.

I need to provide some more details about the phone call since I didn't hear Tom's voice. I never have, California jails don't have telecommunication devices for the deaf (TDDs) so Tom had to call Alex, my hearing neighbor and an acquaintance of both of us. Alex had to keep Tom on hold while he flashed my door lights, wait for me to open the door, and get me to the phone in his apartment. Then he interpreted the call for me.

As I watched Alex sign I inwardly and irrationally cursed the California criminal justice system. It was certainly not reasonable to expect every jail to have a TDD just in case it got a hearing prisoner who needed to call a deaf friend. In California, a jail would probably get one if it had a deaf prisoner, but Tom was behind bars, not me. I didn't want anyone else to know about the call but I had no choice. I don't often wish that I could hear, but this was one of those times.

I trust Alex, basically. Interpreted conversations are supposed to be confidential and I doubted Alex would tell anyone—except his girl friend. This news was too exciting to keep completely to oneself. Alex's girl friend, however, is not one of my favorite people. Knowing her, I also knew that the news of Tom's imprisonment and my trip would be all over campus within a few days. It was easier to tell Alex to tell my boss and some other friends. I preferred everyone to know about Tom openly than in secret. Shit.

I usually look forward to going to the San Francisco Bay area but this plane ride was different. I help people with problems for a living but murder is way over my head. I'm a counselor in a high school, not a detective. I'm good at resolving problems between teachers and students but I've never shot a gun. I'm proficient in basketball and racquetball but I've never practiced the martial arts.

I had no idea who killed Sarah but whoever did was certain to be "tougher" than me. I had promised Tom I'd help but how? I'm usually confident and positive but then I felt inadequate. I'd have communication problems with the police but those I could handle. But a killer? Sarah had been a friend of mine. I might be able to control my anger enough to let me think clearly but what the hell could I *do*? I should have called a lawyer instead of the taxi that took me to the airport.

But I couldn't have. Tom was special to me. He was around to help when Ellen's letter came. He helped me through the worst months of my life. He'd been my friend in need. Now it was my turn. He was not a man to take advantage of friendship or ask for favors. Capable or not, I at least had to be there.

The only part of this mess that didn't surprise me was that it involved Sarah. For as long as I've known him, Tom has had a very specific problem. Women. If one smiles and shows interest in him she becomes a goddess. I liked Sarah too, but convincing him that she had flaws would be like—like getting me to believe that he killed her.

He'd stayed in Berkeley in a job he didn't like just for her. I need to explain that sentence too. It sounds as if they were engaged, living together, or something of the kind. Not so. They'd been lovers for a few months then she'd broken it off. That was over two years ago. He was still hanging around because at the breakup she'd said that "maybe sometime later she'd consider getting together again." See what I mean about Tom?

I assumed that the police already knew about their affair and that she had ended it. I also assumed that they'd interpret that fact differently than I did. To them it would be a motive.

2

The city of Berkeley is a character in this story. I grew up in Manhattan so I'm used to diversity, but Berkeley is something else. If you told me that there was a cult in New York that worshipped tadpoles, I wouldn't believe you. If you said Berkeley, I would. I've eaten an "androgynous ginger being" cookie in Berkeley. Honest.

If there was anything that would work in my favor in helping Tom it would be my analytical and skeptical mind. From the time I could communicate my favorite signs were "who," "what," "where," "when," "how," and especially, "why." (The words came later.) I bugged my parents by wanting to know a reason for everything. An example. I remember asking my mother why forks are set to the left of the plate and spoons and knives to the right. I said it made more sense to put all the silverware on the plate and then let everyone decide for themselves how to arrange their utensils. My mother's only answer, "Because that's the way it's done." was completely unsatisfactory. To give you an idea of what I'm like at 28, I still think my question makes sense and I'm still waiting for an answer.

If any place doesn't make sense and can defy my faith in reason, Berkeley is it. Money, power, jealousy, etc., would be motives for murder in Berkeley but so could lack of proper respect for tadpoles. I'd lived there for a year in 1978 with Ellen then returned to live and work there for four months in 1980. The hippie movement is still alive there, movie theaters serve tiger's milk and zucchini bread instead of popcorn and coke, and there are more bookstores than I can count. In 1980 Tom was my roommate, Sarah a frequent visitor, I liked my job, and I was making plans for a wedding.

Until the dreadful letter came, the beauty and wackiness of the Bay Area was fun. (Neighboring San Francisco is runner-up in the Haven-for-Crazies Bowl) I didn't expect, however, this trip to Berkeley to be fun. I left because there were too many places that reminded me of Ellen. She cancelled our engagement, through the mail, with no reason that I could understand. I had no idea it was coming. The letter hit me like nothing before or since. Tom had to take me to the hospital with attacks of vertigo that were certainly psychosomatic in origin but terrifying nonetheless.

Now I had to go back and face the memories. I felt I'd gotten over Ellen but Berkeley would be the true test. And the craziness would not be fun. I was not flying to California for a vacation. As unreal as it seemed, I was going to solve a murder. Someone had killed a woman I liked and framed my best friend. I was mad.

How the hell was I supposed to think? Berkeley, memories of Ellen, and anger at someone unknown were certain to jumble my emotions. It's nice to be able to solve crossword puzzles, Rubik's cube, and difficult bridge hands with nothing on the line but this was a mystery with Tom's life at stake and I'd be distracted.

As a counselor I'm trained to help others think positively. It was time to use the techniques on myself. As hard as I tried, I could only see one "silver lining." I'd always liked challenges and I was certainly in for one.

3

After I got my suitcase, I needed a car. There was a row of agencies near the baggage claim. Since I'd be charging again I could "afford" any of them. I didn't want to waste time comparison shopping so I decided to see if Avis really did try harder.

"I'd like to rent the smallest and cheapest car you have," I said to the smiling nondescript rental clerk.

"For how long sir?"

Good question. I had no idea but I had to make a decision. "If I take it for a few days can I renew it if I decide to stay longer?"

"Yes, ? ? ? ? ?"

I couldn't catch what he said but I suspected he was quoting me some prices. "Can you write that down for me. I'm deaf and I couldn't understand what you said."

"? ? ? ? ?"

His last words seemed to be "I just told you." I couldn't be sure except that was what his facial expression clearly showed him to mean. I felt like asking him who was deaf, me or him. I've had enough experiences and questioned enough hearing friends to know that I sound as if I have a foreign accent but that my voice is easy to understand. I knew what had happened, it's happened to me many times before. Because I can talk, some people refuse to believe that I can't hear.

When this situation has arisen before my response has varied depending on my perception of the hearing person's attitude. If he or she is just uninformed, I will inform; if the attitude is belligerent, I will lock horns. I felt like battling with

7

this man or switching to another company. However, I was in a hurry and I had murder on my mind.

"Give me the car for a week," I answered.

I picked route 13 for my drive to Berkeley rather than route 17 for nostalgic reasons. It was the way I used to go to work. I wanted to see how I felt retracing my steps after the three intervening years. The first thing that struck me was the beauty.

Part of the soul and magic of the Bay Area is its beauty. Everyone has heard about or seen pictures of the Golden Gate Bridge, the Cable Cars, and the hills that are the streets of San Francisco. But the hills of the East Bay in Oakland and Berkeley are pretty too. The charm is partially man-made since the houses on the slopes are unique and interesting. You don't see town houses or cloned apartments. The homes are individually designed. If you're interested in architecture, go to San Francisco Bay. If you're not, go anyway.

The beauty is natural too. I'd forgotten how green Berkeley was. The hills dominate the city as a verdant frame but the trees, lawns, and even the sidings on many houses throw green all over the canvas. It was early spring but Washington D.C. in mid-summer looks pale in comparison. As I reached the city limits I thought of Ellen.

Perhaps the hills enchanted me, but my musings took an unexpected turn. Her letter wasn't forgotten but I was also seeing our romps through Tilden Park, Golden Gate Park, the Redwood Forests, and Point Reyes National Seashore. When I passed the Claremont Hotel (now the Claremont Resort) I remembered the night we splurged and stayed there. Enough time had passed since the hurt that I could think of both the good and the bad times. Thoughts of Ellen would not distract me. I could concentrate on the matter at hand.

After the Claremont my route shortly brought me to the old California School for the Deaf (C.S.D.) where I'd worked when I was last here. As I drew near I could see that the walls were dingy and several windows were broken. On the gate was an ominous blue sign. The largest letters, the ones I could read first, were the expected NO TRESPASSING. As my car drew closer still I could read another four words. I should have expected them too. The behemoth had commissioned the geological survey that found the small earthquake fault under the school, forcing the poor, vulnerable deaf kids to relocate to Fremont. It was more than a little irritating that the institution that told us our land was unsafe now owned the very same "dangerous" land. The tell-tale words were The University of California.

I parked then walked around the outside surveying the carnage. There was some "construction" going on but all I could see were broken windows, ripped up pavement, and once beautiful buildings in disrepair. The NO TRESPASSING signs didn't keep me out, my general disgust did. After the magic of the hills I was back down to reality.

I got back in the car and headed for a row of motels I knew of on University Boulevard put picked a "scenic" route past the infamous People's Park of the '60s (There was a lot more foliage than when I'd seen it last—the people had apparently been gardening.) and upper Telegraph Ave. (Still full of bookstores, sidewalk vendors, and assorted crazies.) This was the Berkeley I knew.

The only stop I made was at McFarlane's on Shattuck. I'd be likely to need energy for the trip to jail and I couldn't think of a better way to get it than via homemade ice cream. While I was walking with my cone I saw a sign for a curious business establishment—Information on Demand. They claimed to be able to locate or find out whatever you needed to know. I didn't enter. They were a reference outfit, not a detective agency. The only question I needed the answer to was "Who killed Sarah Collins?" If I asked Information on Demand I was sure they could tell me. Tom Hayes. That's what the police said and we all know that the police don't arrest innocent people. Right?

I drove to, and checked in at the Campus Motel. It was small but clean, very ordinary and moderately priced. Since I only intended to use it as a place to sleep and store my luggage it suited me fine. I stayed there just long enough to drop off my bag, then went directly to the jail. (I did not pass Go, I did not collect $200.)

I went inside and followed signs toward the main desk. This time I wanted to be one hundred percent sure of the communication. Misunderstandings at a rental car company can be a hassle but what I'd just experienced was no big deal. But this was a jail and I was dealing with officers of the law. So I took out my trusty pad and pencil.

"My name is Robert Brewer," I wrote. "I'm here to see Tom Hayes. I'm writing to you because I'm deaf."

I could see the officer look at me skeptically. "You're deaf?" I was able to understand that but pretended not to, shook my head, and pointed to my ear. "Wait here," he wrote back.

He left me and came back in five minutes. "Follow me," he wrote. I complied. He led me down a corridor to a set of double doors. There was another officer guarding them and the two said something to each other. My guide left and the new officer led me inside.

The visiting room seemed to be a converted cafeteria, one big open space with twenty pairs of tables laid out in rows. The tables in each pair were bolted to the floor and about three feet from each other. The purpose for this set up was to permit eye-to-eye contact but forbid hand-to-hand contact. There was a guard in each corner of the room. They could see everything but not at the same time. The walls and the ceiling were an institutional off-white and the tiled floor a dingy gray.

My guard led me to a center table then left the room. From a far corner Tom was brought out from another set of double doors to my table. His guard also left but we were hardly alone. There were still the four sentries in the corners and about a dozen other inmate-visitor pairs. I hadn't seen Tom in over a year, since his last visit to D.C. He looked thinner and more haggard. Though he brightened at the sight of me, his depression was apparent.

The normal long-time-no-see handshake was impossible and Hi-what's-up? didn't seem like an appropriate greeting either. "Is the rest of the jail as gloomy as this place?" I found myself beginning.

"Worse."

"No wonder you look so bad."

"Jail I could tolerate, but I can't get Sarah off my mind. I feel like I'm in a daze." I gave a nod of understanding. "Thanks for coming," he added.

"You know I love the Bay Area but this is the weirdest excuse I've ever had for a trip. Anyway, since we have an hour time limit and I intend to get you out of here, I'd better ask you some questions."

"I don't know if I have any answers, but go ahead."

"What happened? How was she killed, where did they find her, etc. etc."

"Her skull was crushed from a blow from one of the marble book ends that she gave me for my birthday. I came home from work at McDonald's, found her lying there all bloody on my bed, screamed, then called 911. I'm not too clear what happened after that. I was in a fog. They questioned me for a short time at my place, for a longer time at the police station, then brought me here."

"Why? Why do they think you did it?"

"She was found in my bedroom. Mine were the only finger prints on the book end and they found out about the argument Sarah and I had had that day during lunch at The Good Earth."

"All circumstantial."

"Yeah, but I can see how from their perspective I look guilty. People have been hung on less evidence."

If we'd been having a normal conversation I'd have expected what came next but I'd been concentrating on the problem at hand. "Guard" Tom said to me and I felt a tap on shoulder. I turned and stared up into the face of one mean looking son-of-a-bitch. "What's going on buddy?"

I knew immediately what was wrong. Tom and I had not been talking. I'm comfortable speaking and signing at the same time but when I'm communicating with someone fluent in American Sign Language (ASL) I drop my voice. I can put English into signs but ASL is a language unto itself. When I speak and sign I must sign English or a pidgin between English and ASL. When I don't speak I can sign English, ASL, pidgin, or combine them or make puns and jokes on how the languages interact and overlap.

I have much more communicative power and more choices availabe to me that way. I can be more creative. Tom's ASL is good so that's how we like to "talk"—without our voices. We can have conversation that's enjoyable as well as informative. Our silence had nothing to do with secrecy but the officers at the jail knew nothing about deafness.

"I'm deaf," I answered, "I explained that to the lieutenant outside."

"If you're talking now, why weren't you talking to him," the guard pointed to Tom, "he's not deaf."

Perhaps I shouldn't have said anything in response to his first question and used pad and pencil as I had at the front desk but I hadn't been thinking and it was too late. I searched for the most servile and submissive tone I could. "I'm sorry officer. I wasn't thinking. As you can probably tell from my voice, I have 'funny' speech and its hard for me. Tom and I will be happy to talk while we sign and you listen. Is that okay with you?"

"I have a lot of people to watch so I can't stand here but I'll be watching from my post and if there's any more funny business I'm tossing you out on your ear."

I didn't catch all of what he'd said (Tom gave me a word for word account later.) but his meaning had been clear.

I continued where Tom and I left off and was careful to speak as clearly as I could. "What was Sarah doing in your bedroom?"

"I don't know."

"How did she get there?"

"She had a key."

"Who else had a key?"

"Only me."

"What about the landlord?"

"Probably, but he lives in Marin County. I never see him. If something breaks I'm supposed to take care of it myself or call a repair man and send him the bill."

12

"Great. What did you and Sarah argue about?"

"The same old thing—us. I asked her to marry me again and again she told me that I could find a better woman. I think we were shouting because we'd said the same things to each other time after time and were trying to make our points sink in. We go out to lunch the first Friday of every month and to dinner every year on my birthday."

He was feeling bad but I had to keep going. At least I could shift the focus a little. "Who had any reason to kill her?

"No one."

"You're a big help."

"You knew her. Everybody loved her."

"Someone apparently didn't."

I don't know why I said such a stupid thing. My display of cleverness brought Tom to tears. My stupidity redoubled my belief in his innocence and my determination to find the real killer. The evidence that was proving Tom guilty had to be shown to be wrong or that it could lead to another conclusion.

How do you know that? has always been a question and subject of interest to me. I knew Tom hadn't killed Sarah but how could I prove it? Ironically, it seems that the more trivial the fact (The Redskins won the Super Bowl.) the easier to prove, the more important (She loves me.) the harder to prove. Tom's innocence was solidly in the she-loves-me category.

"I'm sorry Tom, I shouldn't have said that."

"No," he composed himself and answered, "you're right. But who?"

"That's what I came here to find out."

I got Tom to agree to get a lawyer, then there were still some things I wanted to ask that I preferred for the police not to overhear. I knew that now, among all the conversations going on, we were being singled out for attention. I decided to experiment.

It is easy to sign "yes" and say "no" (or vice versa) at the same time, but anything more than that is difficult, unnatural, and requires practice. I didn't have time to practice but it seemed the most plausible plan.

13

"Where was Sarah working?" I signed while I spoke *"Do you want me to bring some ice cream next time I come?"*

I could see that Tom was puzzled. He depends on his hearing so when I sign and voice simultaneously he doesn't pay much attention to my signs. That's why I spoke something silly and much longer than what I signed. I tried again.

"Where was Sarah working?" I signed while I spoke *"The weather here is nicer than in Washington."*

I saw a gleam in Tom's eyes. He understood. From then on I had no idea of what he said. I had to ignore his silly lip movements and focus solely on the signs. We were both struggling with this odd way of communicating. We were slow and awkward but were having a good time too. I knew that this was no joking matter but still I felt like a school-boy fooling his teacher. Risking the wrath of the guards was a dangerous game to play but that added to the excitement. Tom's facial expressions told me he was feeling the same way.

When our time was up I left knowing what I had to do.

After the long flight, the drive, and the jail I was spent. I had a burger and a beer at a cafe near the motel then went back to my room and hopped into bed with a book. I'd brought my *Hitchhiker's Guide to the Galaxy* and sequels with me just in case I need an antidote to thinking about murder. I was pleased with my foresight since I had the need and the silliness worked. (Example: "In those days spirits were brave, the stakes were high, men were real men, women were real women, and small furry creatures from Alpha Centauri were real small furry creatures from Alpha Centauri.") I was able to get a good night's sleep before my investigation began in earnest.

4

The address Tom gave me was on Telegraph, near Oakland, not far from one of my old haunts, Los Burritos. I'd go there for lunch but first things first. I needed to see Sarah's last place of employment.

The sign on the door said just what Tom had said it would—The Heliotherapy Center of Northern California. If I'd needed a reminder that I was back in Berkeley, I didn't anymore. After all it was Sarah who'd tried, unsuccessfuly, to establish aromatherapy and past lives therapy at California School for the Deaf when it was in Berkeley. Sarah had started a runners group but she was the only one who considered it jogotherapy. From the sign on the door it seemed that she hadn't changed much since I knew her. Except that she was dead.

The office was small: two desks up front, another to the right rear and a partitioned "Director's Office" to the left rear. Near the door there were a few chairs by the closest desk creating what seemed to be an informal waiting area. The walls were papered with dozens of posters of well tanned and well formed young men and women in skimpy swim suits. At first glance, heliotherapy didn't come across as sexist. There were as many pictures of men as of women.

There was only one woman in the office. She was on the phone at the back desk so I picked up one of the brochures laying on a table in the waiting area and read. According to their literature, heliotherapy didn't start in Berkeley, but in Southern California. (No part of the state is immune.) It spread rapidly as its benefits became evident. The central tenet of

15

heliotherapy is that the sun is the source of all life and that by tapping into its energy we can cure all that ails us. The two prime techniques for this communion are "basking" and "tanning." The brochure did not explain the difference between the two. Apparently that requires advanced study.

I didn't think that heliotherapy was for me. I tend to sear or char before I tan. I can accept that the sun is the source of all life on Earth. However, if I weren't investigating a murder I'd have asked if heliotherapy was available to Earthlings who didn't look good in bathing suits. Maybe I'm just a cynic.

My reading was interrupted by a tap on the shoulder. "Can I help you?" the woman who'd been on the phone said and signed simultaneously, and slowly.

Apparently Sarah had still been trying to convert people to deafness too. I could tell from this woman's signs that she was just learning and that it would be almost as easy for me to lip read her, ("Can I help you?" is easy to lip read since you know it's coming.), but I didn't want to discourage her effort so I spoke and signed back to her. "I'm looking for Sarah Collins."

As expected, I flustered her. She didn't know how to tell me that Sarah was dead even though she probably knew the signs and certainly knew the words. As she hesitated, I continued. "I'm an old friend of hers. I live in D.C. now and am on vacation so I thought I'd look her up."

Her discomfort was so acute that I wanted to spare her but that would belie what I'd just said. "Sarah's—dead."

"What?"

"That bastard (she had to fingerspell it, b-a-s-t-a-r-d) killed her. How do you sign bastard?"

I showed her then responded "What?" This time I wasn't feigning surprise. I had never heard anyone refer to Tom as a bastard before. "Who?"

"An ex-boyfriend. Tom Hayes is his name, I think. He couldn't have her so he made sure no one could."

"When?"

"Just last week."

16

"I can't believe it." In a way that was partly true. It was still hard to believe that Sarah was dead and that Tom was in jail even though I'd just visited him there.

As we continued to talk I learned that I was conversing with Nancy Kramer and that she had never actually met Tom, just heard about him. She only volunteered at the Heliotherapy Center, her paying job was at Cody's. Cody's is my favorite bookstore, as comprehensive as any I've ever seen, so we talked about books for a while. (Berkeley and its bookstores is a whole other story.)

The conversation then turned to deafness and sign language. It became apparent that Nancy was another hearing woman I could "catch" through her desire to learn how to sign. Though I'm not proud of it, I've done it several times. Every summer Gallaudet College is flooded with students desiring to learn American Sign Language. They soon find out that the only way to learn is through interacting with deaf people. Finding a deaf "mate" seems to be a popular method of getting that interaction.

Many of the women on the prowl are attractive and I've let myself be caught. None of the relationships lasted. The women were often nice but the problem was me. I didn't like the planned and calculated way I'd behaved so I had to leave.

Yet again I was tempted. Nancy was short but pretty and, of course, well tanned. She could sign a little and I needed information badly. I have a small streak of paranoia in me and it reared its head then too. I think that half the mysteries I've read involve the hero or heroine sleeping with the person who turns out to be the murderer, but what does a murderer look like?

However, my only friend still in Berkeley was in jail and it's nicer not to sleep alone. I asked Nancy to accompany me to Los Burritos for lunch. She accepted.

The burritos were as luscious as I remembered them to be. Nancy wanted to know about me but I tried to steer the conversation to Sarah and the Heliotherapy Center. I could envision it as either an elaborate fraud or another well-intention but simple-minded organization of Californians and californicated people.

From what Nancy told me, fraud seemed remote. There were only three people working at the center, four when Sarah was there. Sarah and the director had been the only paid employees. She'd earned $12,000, he about $15,000. Nancy now had to decide if she wanted Sarah's job or stay at Cody's. The salaries were paid by the home office in Los Angeles which was supported by a private grant. The current projects of the center were to distribute the literature, enlarge the mailing list, and write a book detailing the evidence for heliotherapy's effectiveness. (That, I'll have to read.)

Nancy didn't want to talk about Sarah. She hadn't liked her and now that she'd been murdered she felt guilty about not liking her. Nancy never said that but I could read between the signs. Sarah had been dating both the director, a man named Rudolph Alexis, and the other volunteer whose only known name was Aton. Nancy is an attractive person in every sense of the word but both she and the men at the center compared her to Sarah.

Sarah was not the goddess that Tom thought her to be, but she certainly looked like one. She was five foot eight, slender and shapely, with golden blond hair and golden tan skin. She had a soft smile that attracted men like no other woman I've ever met. If I hadn't been emotionally tied to Ellen when Tom and I first met Sarah I'd probably have chased her too.

And she was smart and witty. No one ever thought of her as a dumb blond. Few men could beat her on the tennis court. The normal male reaction to her was "Wow, what a woman!" Even deaf men who told me they'd never look at a hearing woman chased Sarah.

She had a good heart too but it was all muddled. She couldn't be satisfied with helping the students in her classes at CSD. She was a great teacher but she had to save the world. Every hearing person should know sign language, every person who could walk should jog, every person should examine their past lives, etc.

18

By the time we left the restaurant two hours later Nancy had gotten me to talk enough to find out that I was staying at a motel and secured my agreement to move my things to her place that night. Californians work fast.

5

When we got back from lunch Aton was in the office. Nancy introduced me. Preconceptions are the enemy of sound thinking but they are hard to defeat. I should not have, but from his name I was expecting Aton to be about 6' 4", black, and menacing. Instead, he was 5' 2", white, and dumpy looking.

When Nancy left us to go to her job at Cody's there was an awkward moment of silence. Aton didn't appear to want to converse. It could have been because he didn't know how to talk to a deaf person, because he didn't want to talk to the friend of a woman he'd murdered, or any of a number of other reasons.

I was uncomfortable too. I've had countless non-signed, non-interpreted conversations with hearing people but none like what I wanted with Aton. Until college I shuttled between hearing and deaf schools. I got into minor trouble wherever I went. The deaf schools were excruciatingly boring. The public schools I tried seemed to be blessed with teachers who lectured while writing on the blackboard, changing the exhaustingly difficult task of lip-reading to an impossibility.

So, I'm a good lip-reader but had had no experience interrogating a murder suspect via lip-reading. I went ahead from a lack of any other option. I could sense that Aton would have even less patience than I with a written conversation.

"I can't believe it about Sarah," I said. "Was she a friend of yours too?"

"Yes."

"Do you think that the guy they have locked up really killed her?"

"Yes."

"Did you know him?"

"No."

I'm nearly infallible at understanding "yes" and "no" still I didn't feel that I'd uncovered a promising method of investigation. This was not turning out to be much of an inter-rogation. My clever tack of innocence and friendliness didn't seem to be much of a hit.

"Nancy's a nice woman, isn't she?"

"Yes."

"Well, it's been nice to meet you."

"Yes."

We shook hands and I left the heliotherapy center feeling like a fool.

If I were a proper detective I should have (at least according to the literature) gone straight to a bar. I enjoy social drinking but alcohol does nothing to improve my thinking, and I needed to think. Instead of a pub I found Eclair. Carbohydrates probably don't help my mentation either but I always search for excuses to savor black forest cake, tortes, chocolate cheese cake, and the like.

It was three o'clock in the afternoon and I wasn't due at Nancy's till ten. I meant to continue my work but was not up to struggling with another hearing suspect so I drove thirty miles south to Fremont and the new C.S.D. Tom's current woman friend taught school there. He was dating other women because Sarah had ordered him to. He was collecting evidence to disprove her assertion that he could find a better woman for him than her. I wondered if his dates knew that.

The traffic on route 17 was heavy, as always, but as a New Yorker, that doesn't bother me. Manhattan streets and the Cross Bronx Expressway aren't just crowded, they're tests of survival. I'd never been to the new school, but with a map I found it easily.

C.S.D. Berkeley had been a pretty school. I was imme-diately impressed because so was C.S.D. Fremont. The parking lot was filled with daisies in bloom. The East Bay hills were still there providing the picturesque green background. The buildings were small and homey, built mostly or completely of wood. Students live there week days but there are no "dorms." When I used that sign I was quickly corrected. Students live, 24 per building, in "cottages."

When I got out of the car the scent of the daisies assaulted me pleasantly. The atmosphere was fresh and alive. I could see staff and students just meandering while enjoying the California sun. Younger children were at play.

But to me the nicest sights were the flying hands. Everyone was signing. Many people were talking too (I could see lips moving) but everyone was signing. I wouldn't have to struggle to read lips and guess at meanings. I could communicate without barriers. It was so relaxing an environment that it almost made me forget about murder. But not quite.

I stopped a student at random and got directions to the high school and Ms. Grafton's classroom. Charlotte was still there. She was 5' 4", with short black hair, stocky, but not fat. I didn't find her either attractive or plain but I wasn't there to pick her up.

The "deaf world" is a small one and the deaf professional world even smaller. It was unusual, therefore, that I'd never met Charlotte even though we grew up a continent apart. We were approximately the same age. After talking for a few minutes I found out the reason. She was one of the few deaf intellectuals who had never made the pilgrimmage to Gallaudet. She was a native Oregonian who got both her B.A. and M.A. at CSUN (California State University at Northridge) then found her job at C.S.D. Fremont.

I told her who I was, why I'd come to California, and that I'd come to see her because she'd been seeing Tom. I made it clear that I had no objections to deaf women dating hearing men because I have no objections and I wanted to start off on the right foot with her. I wanted information but I didn't plan to tell her that she was one of my suspects.

"If you're a friend of Tom's," she told me, "that means you're a friend of mine but how could you have liked her, the way she used him."

"When I knew her they were sweethearts. What do you mean?"

"Sweethearts is fine, but when a woman leaves a man she should leave him. She kept him dangling on a string ever since. I wish she'd just gone away instead of getting herself murdered."

"You don't think he killed her?"

"Of course not, I love him."

Since I agreed with her I refrained from pointing out that her conclusion did not follow from her premise.

"Do you have any idea who did?" I asked.

"No, but let me know when you find him so I can thank him. Once you get Tom out of jail he'll see that unlike her, I'm a woman who knows a good man when she sees one."

I left the classroom and walked around the campus to see if I could find any old friends. Thank "him" Charlotte had said. It's true that most murders are committed by men but if Nancy and Charlotte were representative, Sarah hadn't been too popular with other women. "Once you get Tom out of jail" Charlotte had also said. She was more confident of that than I was.

I found a few Gallaudet buddies working in the dorms and joined them for dinner in the CSD cafeteria. Usually the sentence "When you've seen one you've seen them all." is a stupid thing to say. However, when it comes to cafeterias at residential schools for the deaf, it's basically true. The physical settings vary but the slop they serve doesn't. At least I'd recently come from both Los Burritos and Eclair.

After catching up on the California news and sharing the D.C. dirt I went to Berkeley. The reunion had been a necessary relaxing interlude but my sleuthing was far from over. I still had no answers to "Who?", "How?", or "Why?".

24

I checked out of the motel and found Nancy's place without too much difficulty. She actually lives in Oakland but just a hop, skip, and a jump (literally) from Berkeley. The logical part of my mind told me that there was nothing significant to the name of the street where she lived but there are other-than-rational parts of my brain. Alcatraz Street. (Yes, with a view of the island.) Alcatraz is no longer a prison, just a tourist attraction. Still, the street sign was an unpleasant reminder of what Tom's fate would be if I failed and an uneasy omen regarding the suspect I was about to move in with.

Nancy's apartment building was small, just two floors, about ten or twelve apartments in all. Even in the poor illumination from the street lights I could see that it was an ordinary building. The walls were gray concrete, the shape a plain rectangle. In another area of the country it would be unremarkable, here that very trait made it unusual.

Nancy opened the door when I rang the bell. (I didn't hear it but I assumed it rang since my pushing the button summoned her. Though I have a few friends who are "stone-deaf", it is a rare condition. I'm pretty close but there are four sounds that I can recognize easily: fireworks, jet plane take-offs, loud rock music, and the New York City subways. Aren't I lucky?) I barely had a chance to step inside and put down my bags when she kissed me and asked "How was your afternoon?"

I had many possible ways to respond to that question in light of what had happened. The things I had to keep foremost in mind were that Nancy still didn't know the real reason for my trip and that I had just met her that afternoon, (despite the wife-like nature of her question and embrace.)

"Fine," I answered. "How was work?"

"The usual. Neither boring nor exciting. Do you want a glass of wine?"

"That sounds great."

"Why don't you take your bags to the bedroom. I'll bring the wine there."

The inside of Nancy's place was quite different from the banality of the outside. The most notable feature of her apartment was an absence. There was no living room. There should have been, or at least the architect had intended there to be one. Nancy had, however, used book shelves, wine racks, and a bar to create two separte areas. Depending on your choice of words they could be called a lounge and a library, or a bar and a den. Whatever, the effect was clear. One room said this is where I read; the other, this is where I drink. The kitchen and dining room were also separate. This is where I cook; this is where I eat. Accepting Nancy's suggestion I didn't tarry in any of the above. I went to the bedroom.

The theme there was also evident. There was a small bookshelf containing Cleland's original *Fanny Hill*, Erica Jong's *Fanny*, *The Joy of Sex*, *How to Make Love to a Man*, *How to Make Love to Each Other*, etc. The walls were postered with "hunks." There were no chairs or other extraneous furniture, only a king size waterbed. I sat down on the edge of the bed.

When she brought the wine and sat beside me I felt it incumbent upon me to confess. I had no idea how long I'd be staying. "Fine" would soon become an inadequate answer to her questions, I didn't want to worry about continually inventing plausible lies, and I wanted to tell her.

I was not Sherlock Holmes in need of a Dr. Watson but it helps to share your thoughts with and bounce your ideas off someone else. Explaining often helps me think more clearly about what I'm explaining. There is an inner price to keeping one's thoughts constantly inside and I didn't want to pay it. I also have to admit that in the back of my mind was the feeling that a hearing person who could sign could come in handy. I hadn't forgotten my wonderful talk with Aton.

"Nancy," I started, "I have a confession to make."

"You're gay."

In the bay area that's a very natural question to ask. "No, not at all. I'll be ready to ravish you as soon as I finish my story. It's just that I'm not here on vacation."

"If you're looking for a job that's fine too. You're welcome to stay as long as you like."

"No. I do work in D.C. and I was a friend of Sarah's. But the reason I came out here was because Tom called me. We were roommates when I lived here three years ago and were friends before that. He asked me for help because he says he didn't kill her and I believe him."

"Then who did?"

"That's what I'm here to find out. That's what I was trying to do this afternoon except that I found out almost nothing."

"Wow. You're even more exciting a man than I thought.'

She took both of our glasses, put them on the floor, then knocked us prone onto the undulating surface of the bed. It was quite a while before there was any more talk of murder, or any talk at all.

6

Occasionally I've been asked to compare deaf and hearing women in bed. It's hard to respond. I'm sure I've not sampled enough of either to make a statistically valid comparison, and my subjective impressions don't point to any generalizations. Nancy had been energetic and insistent whereas Ellen was a clinger and cuddler. Their erotic characteristics meshed with their daytime personalities but didn't seem to correlate with their respective ability to discriminate sound. It was a subject, however, that would be much more enjoyable to investigate than Sarah's murder.

I thought about what I'd accomplished so far and it wasn't a pleasant review. I'd met three of the four people I considered suspects. I didn't want the killer to be Nancy. I liked her. I was going back to D.C. as soon as I was finished but would probably come back to the Bay Area from time to time. If Nancy was innocent I'd have an inviting place to stay. If she were guilty she'd go to jail and I wouldn't be able to stand the thought of our time together. One choice was obviously more desirable to me.

I hadn't particularly liked Charlotte but I didn't want her to be guilty either. It wasn't because of her professed love for Tom, it was her deafness. That may sound bad to some people, but I am deaf and I didn't relish the idea that one of "us" may have killed someone. No matter how dissimilar we are, there is something about hearing loss that creates a common bond. Cultural differences, personal enmity, and other factors can overpower it, but it's still there.

Aton was the third suspect and I knew very little about him. He didn't like talking to me but there are many people in that category and none that I know of are murderers. I knew from Nancy that Aton had taken responsibility for the mailing lists at the heliotherapy center. It was a seemingly innocuous and boring job. Nancy said he'd been dating Sarah though I couldn't see what had interested her.

I also assumed that he was not using his given name. Aton was the ancient Egyptian god of the sun. It seemed too apt a name for someone volunteering at a "heliotherapy" center. It didn't feel right but my unease was hardly something I could bring to the police without getting laughed at. I would have to find a way to learn more about him.

I hoped he'd be at the center when I went back that morning but my first priority was to see the last suspect on my list—Rudolh Alexis, the director of the Heliotherapy Center of Northern California, the man who was writing the book that would provide evidence for heliotherapy's effectiveness. Nancy expected him to be there in the morning. I hoped so because in the afternoon I wanted to go back to C.S.D. There were some more questions I needed to ask Charlotte.

After the loving, Nancy and I had talked. I asked her to tell me anything she remembered that might help. She didn't know much about Sarah's relations with Aton and Alexis except that they knew about each other. She also assumed that neither relationship was platonic. She tried to hide her resentment about that but didn't succeed too well.

The other piece of information that she thought was significant was that Sarah had had a heated argument at the center with a deaf woman just two days before her death. Nancy had no idea what the argument was about since they had both signed without voice and rapidly. She knew it had been an argument from the stares, glares, and other facial expressions. Nancy was upset that she "hadn't understood a single sign." Until then she'd been happy with her progress learning sign language. I promised to continue to teach her and told her that understanding arguments would be the last thing to come. After

I soothed her a little, I asked her to describe the other woman. No doubt about it. Charlotte.

Except that he was white, "Rudy" Alexis fit the image that I had incorrectly conjured up for Aton, who was not around. I made a mental bet that Rudy had played tight end or power forward for somebody. Nancy introduced me as an old friend of Sarah's and a new friend of hers who was interested in learning about heliotherapy. I explained that I was deaf and that I'd try to lip read him but if I didn't understand something I'd ask Nancy to sign it for me.

He said that was fine and began a monologue starting with his life history. During the first few minutes I had to ask for Nancy's help several times but after I got the drift of what he was saying and became accustomed to his speech I needed her less and less. That "interrogation" went smoothly, so much so that it was quite a while before I needed to ask questions.

Rudy grew up in San Francisco and was an abused and neglected child, abused by his father and neglected by his mother. He was always in fights. He said that he could never ignore an insult and always lashed out violently. He credited football and basketball (I was right on both counts.) with letting him vent off enough energy to let him get through high school without being expelled or arrested by the police.

The turning point in his life came, he claimed, during his junior year at U.C. Berkeley, when he found heliotherapy. He'd tried dozens of other therapies during his first two years but had made only "superficial and transitory" progress. A.H. (I lip read that, A.H., clearly but had to ask him what he meant— After Heliotherapy) he got in touch with his true self and graduated with honors.

For the three years since his graduation he'd been directing the center and working on his book, which he called his "labor of love." A large portion of the book would be his own case history. Other chapters would detail the salvation of other individuals. There'd be chapters on the theoretical foundations and the statistical validations of heliotherapy, but he hadn't started on those yet.

31

I told him I was looking forward to reading it. In Northern California I had no doubt he'd be able to find a publisher.

Changing the subject, I said that I was amazed at how Sarah had always been able to balance men, that Nancy had told me that she'd been dating both him and Aton. My comment didn't faze him at all.

"Aton and I always knew that. Sarah was not a secretive person," he answered. "I'm sure that many other men were chasing her, so I wouldn't be surprised if there wasn't someone else in the running with us too. Between Aton and I it was friendly competition. Like one-on-one basketball."

Bullshit! I wanted to say. Friendly competition is certainly possible in basketball, but for Sarah's affections I didn't believe it, especially since she'd been murdered and Tom had been framed.

"I understand," I lied. "As long as I knew her there'd always been competition for her." The last part was true.

"She was a rare woman."

"That's for sure." I could sense Nancy's discomfort. Time to switch topics again. "By the way, I'm just curious, what's Aton's real name.

"Aton, as far as I know."

"What about job applications, tax forms, etc?"

"He's a volunteer. It would be silly to question or risk alienating free labor."

"True, but how does he eat? I mean how does he earn a living?"

"I never asked."

"I see. It was nice to meet you. I don't know how long I'll be staying but I hope to see you again. In any case I want a copy of your book as soon as it's off the presses."

"You've got it."

"Autographed?"

"Sure thing."

"Thanks for talking to me."

"It's been my pleasure."

32

As I drove to Fremont I tried to sort out my impressions of Rudy Alexis. He was open and friendly. He seemed to be a true believer in heliotherapy but his comments about Sarah had been all too casual. I knew her and she couldn't be taken that way. She was dynamic and charismatic. Whether you were her lover, friend, enemy, or just acquaintance, she "hit" you. Being blasé about her would be like being indifferent to a typhoon. Rudy's attitude toward Aton bothered me too but it was a feeling that I couldn't pin down. All in all, the interview had gone as well as I could expect. I'd gotten a lot of information.

When I got to C.S.D. and found Charlotte I got straight to the point. I explained that she'd been seen having a set-to with Sarah at the heliotherapy center just two days before she died.

"So," Charlotte answered.

"Why didn't you tell me yesterday?"

"I didn't think it was any of your business."

"I thought you wanted Tom out of jail?"

"I do."

"How the hell am I supposed to do that if his friends cover up or give me half-truths. Whoever killed him will certainly be lying. So, if you don't mind, what were you and Sarah arguing about?"

"Tom."

"Thanks for the startling revelation. Could you spare me a few more details?"

"I told her to get out of his life. She said they were friends and she wouldn't give up the only true friend she'd ever had just because some other woman was jealous. I told her that if she were really his friend she'd leave him so that he could find another woman. She said Tom wanted their lunch dates as much as she did. I told her that she had to be some kind of mean bitch to want to keep on hurting a 'friend' of hers. She may have said something after that but I don't know because I got up and walked out. Is that what you wanted to know? Are you satisfied now?"

"I'm satisfied that you're telling the truth."

"I'm so happy to hear that."

"If you think of anything else call me at this number." I wrote it down and handed it to her. "You'll have to find an interpreter. The person I'm staying with is hearing and doesn't have a tdd."

"Person. I bet that 'person' is a woman. I see you haven't let your concern for Tom interfere with your pleasures."

"If you're what Tom has to look forward to when he gets out, he might be better off in jail. But don't worry. I'll free him so you can show him how sweet a woman you are."

"Bastard."

"When I'm provoked. Thank you for your time."

I stopped at a Taco Bell on the way home, I mean Nancy's place, to eat and think. I'd met all my suspects. All had a motive—the same one for all four, the same one the police attributed to Tom—jealousy. However, simple jealousy does not a murderer make. I've been jealous often in my life and so has most everyone I know. The motive would have to be tied into a murderous personality in a complex way that I had yet to discover.

The next piece of the puzzle to attack was opportunity. Who could have committed the crime, who didn't have an alibi? The police hadn't asked anyone and I couldn't, not directly. Aton wouldn't talk to me and Charlotte was unlikely to after our recent chat. Nancy and Rudy were friendly to me but I could hardly ask either of them "What were you doing the night of the murder?" If I was to find out I'd have to do a lot better job at being subtle than I'd been so far. It was obvious I had a lot to learn about detection.

On the agenda for the morrow was a meeting with Tom, then, if possible, Tom's lawyer. I hoped he could help with more than just the law but I'd have to decide that when I met him. The one thing I knew I wanted from him was to get me in to the scene of the crime to see what I could see.

I do not have x-ray vision. No deaf person does. I test at the standard 20-20 but I do notice more than most hearing people do. Most of my information about the world comes through my eyes so I use them better. Perhaps I'd see something in Tom's apartment that the police overlooked or weren't looking for. Maybe not, but I had to try. I'd have a different motivation behind my eyes than the police had had when they answered Tom's call.

When I arrived "home" Nancy was there with her welcoming hug.

"How did it go this afternoon?" she asked.

"Wonderfully. I found out what I already knew and made an enemy."

"What do you mean?"

"Charlotte admitted that she and Sarah had quarreled about Tom but resented my prying. I resented her lack of cooperation so we didn't part as best of friends."

"Oh. I see. Anyway, enough talk about murder. Let's go to Grand Central."

"Isn't it a little far and a little crowded?"

"We may have to wait but it's very private. And it's only ten minutes from here."

"Unless you know how to teleport, we're talking about two different places. Grand Central Station is 3,000 miles away in Manhattan and it's often used as the archetype of crowdedness."

"Not Grand Central Station, silly, Grand Central Hot Tubs."

"Oh. I've never been there."

"Then we have to go."

"Sounds good to me. What do I have to bring?"

"Just your body."

"That sounds even better."

"Each room has a built in shower, sauna, bed, and AM-FM radio, as well as the tub, towels are provided," the clerk said. "It's $14.50 an hour for two." I didn't ask Nancy to interpret. Lip reading is easy when the information someone is reciting is posted on the wall behind her.

"Fine," I said.

"That'll be $14.50."

"No." I grinned at Nancy and spoke to the clerk. "$29."

"Two hours," she said. "I'll ring your room ten minutes before your time is up." Nancy giggled and poked me in the ribs. It was hard to part with so much of my dwindling cash (they don't accept plastic) but that's what I get for acting cool.

I could say quite a lot about those two hours but most would be a digression from my story and shocking to many non-Californians. Suffice it to say that we didn't turn on the radio but turned each other on in the tub, sauna, shower, and bed. I recommend a visit to California's Grand Central, not New York's.

The only talk worth mentioning was my request for Nancy to set up a racquetball game between Rudy and I for the following evening. She agreed. I was to check at the heliotherapy center during the day to see if she'd been successful.

I'd never had as enjoyable a two hour dalliance but Charlotte's taunt stuck in my mind. I had not come to California for sex. As hard as Grand Central Hot Tubs made it, I had to remember that.

7

"How well do you know Charlotte?" I asked Tom. "What kind of relationship do you have?" We were back at the visiting tables at the jail, this time using our voices while we signed.

"We've been dating for about three months. She's a teacher at C.S.D."

"You've already told me that and I've already met her. I mean what is she like under that bitchy shell, or is that really her? Remember I'm trying to find a killer."

"It couldn't have been Charlotte. She isn't a killer and she isn't bitchy at all. She's sweet and kind."

I was about to say something sarcastic when I realized that this was *Tom* I was talking to. I needed to concentrate on finding the murderer, not waste my time in a futile attempt to a get a realistic appraisal of a woman from Tom. If I wanted to obtain information about sweet, lovable Charlotte I'd have to try more direct questions.

"Were you sleeping with her?" I asked.

"Yes."

"Your face and your weak sign seem to say that you're embarrassed about it."

"I am."

"Why?"

"I don't love her."

"I know that but you've slept with other women you didn't love without qualms."

"But she loves me."

"Or so she says. Have you told her you love her?"

"No."

"So where's this guilt coming from?"

"It's a good thing she can't hear. If she could she'd hate me."

"I don't understand. I asked you about guilt and you're a hearing person."

"No, no. This isn't a deaf-hearing issue. It's just that the last time we slept together I found myself calling out Sarah's name right in the middle of intercourse. It's a good thing Charlotte couldn't hear what I said. That's all."

"Tom, do yourself a favor. After you get out of jail, go join a monastery. You and women don't mix. You're going to get yourself killed."

"Maybe you're right."

"No, I'm not right, but we'll work on that problem later. Now we have to get you out of this depressing place. Did you get a lawyer like I asked, tell him what I needed, and arrange for him to meet with me."

"Yes." His name is Russell Jefferson. He works for the public defender's office. He believes me too."

"Then we should get along. When do I get to see him?"

"At one this afternoon at a coffee shop on Durant. He'll be on the run and can only spare a few minutes. He says he'll be easy to recognize. If there's more than one black man there he'll be the only one wearing a suit and tie."

"I'll find him."

One of the facts that is hard to reconcile with my logical mind is how large a part luck and coincidence play in our lives. My mother is from the Mid-West and was on a three day tour of New York when she literally bumped into my father in the subway. Not only were they both deaf, they both had the identical type of genetic deafness, insuring that all their children would be deaf. In the car accident where my brother broke both his legs, a fraction of a second one way or the other would have left him dead or completely unhurt.

Of course there are millions of examples but the one of particular relevance here is how different this story would be if, on the way from the jail to the heliotherapy center, I hadn't decided that I was in the mood for another eclair. The one I'd had two days before had been so luscious.

If I hadn't gone back to Eclair my peripheral vision would not have taken in what I saw through the window of the nearby Kwique Copy Center. If I hadn't been strolling while savoring the cream filling I wouldn't have seen Aton waiting on line inside. If I had had to wait on line myself at the bakery I wouldn't have seen him hand a copy of the heliotherapy mailing list (The blazing sun letterhead was unmistakable) to the man at the counter to be copied at the prevailing Berkeley price of 3½¢ a page.

That fortune, or misfortune, produced profound consequences. I left the area quickly so that Aton wouldn't see me and drove straight to the heliotherapy center. Nancy and Rudy were both there. Rudy was happy that I'd suggested a racquetball game. He said that he was looking forward to it and asked me to meet him back at the office at 6:00. I apologized to Nancy for being unable to join her for lunch or dinner because of business and said that I'd see her later in the evening. She told me not to worry. She'd be waiting for me whenever I got home. When I left for my meeting with Russell Jefferson, Aton had not yet returned.

I was eager to meet Russell Jefferson. He had a sense of humor. He obviously hadn't picked our meeting place at random. The name of the coffee shop was Sufficient Grounds. Cute.

Sufficient Grounds was undistinguished in decor. There was an order for yourself counter and old but not antique tables and chairs. The menu was chalked in on several black-boards around the single room. The cafe was notable, however, via its aromas. Every variety of coffee I had ever heard of, and more, was being imbibed. It was a heady mixture. I was settled with a croissant and a superb cup of cappucino when Jefferson walked in.

I can sum up my first impression of him in one word— distinguished. Possibly because Tom had said he worked for public defender's office, I expected a young man. I was wrong.

He was at least fifty but his beard and natural hair fit him well. Without any information other than his appearance and attire I would have pegged him as a judge, not just a lawyer. Before I rose to greet him I was glad he was on our side. He joined me without ordering.

"I'm Bob Brewer, happy to meet you, Mr. Jefferson." He reached across the table and shook my hand. We sat down. "Well," I continued, "do they have sufficient grounds to keep Tom in jail?"

"Yes." He ignored my attempt at levity. I seemed to be wrong about the sense of humor but I couldn't argue with his desire to get straight to business. "I have a copy of the police report you requested." He handed a folder to me. Next he gave me an envelope. "This letter authorizes you to act as an investigator for me. Bring it to Sergeant Grimsley at the main police station. She's expecting you this afternoon. She'll accompany you to Mr. Hayes' apartment and stay while you look around."

I hadn't caught the name of the officer while he talked to me but her name was written on the envelope. "Thank you," I answered. "I hope I can find out something to help us."

"I hope so too. Your friend convinced me of his innocence but the evidence against him is strong. I'm not immediately worried because I have many manoeuvers I can use to delay the trial. A year, if necessary."

"I don't think I'll have a job waiting for me back East if I stay here a year."

"I have accepted Mr. Hayes' case and will seek to defend him to the best of my ability. Your assistance is appreciated, but I will continue regardless."

"Thank you. My job and my boss in Washington are my problem. I'm glad we're working together, but I would like to solve this case quickly."

"That's understandable."

"Tom told me you were pressed for time so I won't keep you. The last thing I want to talk to you about is alibis. I have four potential suspects but it would be awkward for me to ask them about their whereabouts."

"Give me the names and the addresses. I will ask, as Mr. Hayes' attorney, for formal statements from all of them. Your name will not be mentioned."

"Thank you." I wrote out the list for him using C.S.D. as the address for Charlotte and the heliotherapy center for Rudy and Aton.

"Here's my card. I am hard to reach and since you can't use the phone you can stop by my office and leave any information for me with my secretary. She has instructions to provide you with copies of everything from my files that you need."

"Thank you again Mr. Jefferson."

"You're welcome."

I'd read the police report in the car before I went in the station but I wasn't fully prepared for Sergeant Grimsley. I'd caught Jefferson's "she" when he mentioned her but I wasn't expecting a 5'10" well-proportioned red head with a smile. (Don't ask me what I was expecting. I don't know.) She wasn't pretty enough to be one of Charley's Angels nor did she have the image. She was polite but her manner spoke more of police officer than woman. That was fine with me. To see the scene of the crime what I needed was a police officer. I gave her Jefferson's letter and she led the way.

Tom lived on McGee near Addison in a residential area several blocks west of the university and downtown. Like most of Berkeley's neighborhoods it was middle class and had a patchwork quality. The houses were close together and they varied in no discernable pattern except that none were tall. One house was ornate, the next plain; one was fenced in, one not. One had solar collectors on the roof, another had a big picture of Donald Duck painted on the side. Standard Berkeley.

Like Nancy, Tom lived in a two-story apartment building. As a New Yorker it's hard to think of anything that small as an apartment building. If it's less than five floors it's even called a "walk-up." I grew up in a 12th floor apartment overlooking the Hudson and my brother lives on the 36th floor of a building overlooking the East River. But New York is as abnormal in its own way as Berkeley is. I had to remind myself to think Californian.

Tom's building was odd in that the end faced the street. To get to the length of the building and the apartment doors you had to walk through two palms and two live oaks. (That nomenclature doesn't make sense to me. I know that live oaks are different from plain old oak trees. English can be a strange language sometimes. Imagine having to describe one of those trees after being struck by lightning. It would become a "dead live oak.") Point one to remember—Tom's apartment was in the middle of the second floor, invisible to the street.

Sergeant Grimsley led the way up the stairs and opened the door for me. She guarded the entrance while I investigated. On the way she'd told me that I was free to touch and probe the apartment as I pleased but that I could take nothing out.

It was a one bedroom-one bath with white walls and ceiling and a dark brown wooden floor. The kitchen had room for a small table and four chairs. The living room was moderately sized, about 18 by 15. There was no separate dining room.

The most striking feature of the apartment, to me at least, was its reflection of Tom's personality. The living room had hundreds of books, a T.V. and a sofa bed. (Californians should always be prepared for out-of-town visitors.) The kitchen had the bare minimum of utensils and dishes. The bedroom had a queen-size bed, a dresser, a small walk in closet, and hundreds more books—a love that Tom and I share.

The walls of both the living and bed rooms were decorated with pictures from Sierra Club calendars. If I remember right, Sarah was a member and gave Tom and other friends Sierra Club calendars every year for Christmas. Despite the pictures it was obvious that Sarah had not been living with Tom. Amid all the books there were not only no health food cookbooks, there were no cookbooks at all. Sarah's library had been chock full of two categories that Tom and I ignored, cooking and self-help.

Even more telling was the single house plant sitting on the kitchen window sill. I'd lay odds that Sarah had brought it.

Tom couldn't be bothered with them. When I'd visited Sarah's place three years ago it looked like a jungle.

(Sarah got mad at me then for suggesting a simple experiment in communication. She said she talked to her plants. I suggested that she divide her plants into four groups. Group one, the control, she wouldn't communicate with at all. Group two she should talk to. To group three she should talk and sign simultaneously. To group four she should sign without her voice. Based on the assumption that plants would grow better under the communication mode they preferred, she should measure the growth of all four groups over time. I said that for all we knew she could find out that, unbeknownst to her, she might have a deaf plant or two. I can't understand why not, but she didn't adopt my proposal.)

Among all Tom's books there was one section that struck me as unusual. They were sprawled like a bunch of fallen dominoes on the dresser near the bed. They were all about management and business; *Theory Z*, *The Art of Japanese Management*, *Looking Out for Number One*, etc. He'd had none of them when we'd been roommates and working at C.S.D. but before his arrest he'd been working as night manager at McDonald's. I know he prefers to read fiction so the books on the dresser told me he was trying to do the best he could at his job.

It was hopeless, of course. He is nearly as inept at organization and commanding staff as he is at managing women. Like me, he was a counselor. He belonged in counseling with the deaf but their wasn't a job for him in his field in Berkeley when C.S.D. moved and Berkeley was Sarah's adopted and spiritual home. (She grew up in Sacramento but didn't like to admit it.) As I said before, he'd stayed in Berkeley for Sarah. When I got him out of jail I'd have to get him out of Berkeley and back to where he was needed.

It wasn't, however, the topic of his bedside books that struck me as most wrong. It was their position. I'd roomed with Tom. He was neither messy nor fastidious but his books were always in order. They placed tightly on a shelf from one end to the other, stacked neatly in piles, or sandwiched between bookends. Bookends. Tom had told me that Sarah had been killed with *one* of the bookends Sarah had given him. Tom's finger-prints had been on it.

I flipped through the police report Jefferson had given me, checking my memory. I was right. The police had confis-cated one bookend, the assumed murder weapon. Dummies. Didn't they know that bookends came in pairs?

I opened every closet, crawled under the bed, shook the sheets and pillows that were still caked with dried blood. I spent over an hour and missed no inch of the apartment. No second bookend.

Sergeant Grimsley must have been bored but waited patiently. I was engrossed in my search and made no effort to communicate with her. When I was finally finished she drove me back to the police station and I walked to my own car feeling a little better about my ability as a detective. I'd seen something the police hadn't. They thought they were in posession of the murder weapon but I knew better.

I had over an hour left before I was slated to meet Rudy so I went to The Good Earth to celebrate with champagne and the best carrot cake west of the Hudson. I'm not sure how, but the mixture of the two ended my euphoria. As soon as I began to think lucidly I realized that my perspicacity at Tom's apart-ment was not so thrilling a development in this case as my temporary insanity had led me to believe.

I was fairly certain what had happened. Whoever had killed Sarah with one bookend had probably pocketed it. The next step would be to pick up the other bookend with a cloth or towel or anything handy, rub it in the wound, and leave it by the body. A neat theory. It made sense and all I had to do to prove it would be to find the missing bookend.

Great. Finding a bookend in Berkeley would be like locating the proverbial needle in a haystack. Except that I had a very good idea where the bookend was and it was not Berke-ley. I was operating on the assumption (a good one, I think) that the killer did not want to be caught. (No one had stepped forward to absolve Tom.) He or she, therefore, would not want the bookend to be found. If I were that killer I could think of a safe repository without difficulty.

I wouldn't even bother to ask. What would you say if you were the police and got a request to dredge San Francisco Bay?

8

Rudy was alone when I got to the heliotherapy center. Nancy would be at work at Cody's and Aton who knows where.

"Are you ready to lose?" Rudy asked.

"I'm ready to play."

"That's the same thing. Where are you parked?"

"Right out front at a meter."

"I'm around the corner. I'll pull around, honk, then you can follow me."

"Thanks, but that won't work. I won't be able to hear your horn."

"Sorry. It's hard to remember that you really can't hear anything."

"That's okay. I can't hear, but I can play racquetball."

"We'll see about that. My car is a black MGB. I'll pull up even with you so you can see me."

"You catch on fast."

"I try."

Rudy's club was twenty minutes away in San Leandro, which borders Oakland on the south as Berkeley does on the north. Rudy drove gently, making it easy for me to follow him. It wasn't what I expected from an MGB owner but I think he was trying to be considerate of my deafness even though it's no handicap at all when tailing someone by automobile. Staying behind him wasn't even a challenge.

Californians seem to like legal puns. Earlier in the day I'd supped at Sufficient Grounds. Rudy's racquetball club was named The Supreme Court. I couldn't help but wondering if something more than just a racquetball game would be decided there. It was, after all, why I'd asked for the game in the first place. I wanted to get to know my suspects better. Direct questioning was only one approach. I didn't know what I'd learn from Rudy via racquetball but athletic competition creates a kinship and fellow-feeling between men. Shared sweat and strain often loosens tongues and intimacies are revealed—especially concerning women. Relationships between men and women were clearly the key to this case. If worst came to worst, I'd learn nothing but get some exercise to balance my eclairs, burritos, etc.

I won the first ten points of the first game. Too easily. Rudy was big, strong, fast, and experienced at racquetball. I play well but I could see from the warm up that he was more than my equal. He wasn't a pro or completely out of my class, but a player whose size and power would give him an edge over me.

The first ten points, therefore, were abnormal and I knew it. Rudy wasn't consciously playing weakly or throwing the game but he was overconfident. I'm only 5'8", 180. I'd have to prove to him that I was competition before he would really play. I did and he did.

The next thirty points were some of the best and most exhausting I've ever played. Rudy displayed all his skill and strength and won 19 of the 30, but I had that opening 10 point gift. I squeaked by 21-19.

It would be inaccurate to say that Rudy was mad. He didn't seem to blame me, but he couldn't accept that he'd lost. He only said one word to me and lip reading had never been easier. "Again" had been clear on his mouth and ferocious on his face. It wasn't a Jekyll-Hyde transformation, rather a frightening intensification of his basic personality. I didn't even consider declining the rematch.

Almost needless to say, I didn't win that game nor the next. I managed 11 points in game two and 13 in game three and earned every one of them. I would have been happy to quit after the second game but I could see Rudy wasn't. At that point

48

we were tied one-to-one in games. A simple revenge for my initial victory wasn't enough. He had to win the series, which he did.

After the games were over we showered then relaxed in the sauna and jaccuzi. Rudy was back to the mellow, friendly man I talked to earlier. Despite the goodwill I wasn't comfortable in the sauna. I hadn't forgotten that he was one of my suspects. There I was all alone, completely naked, in a small dark room with this bull of a man who had just humiliated me in a sport I play well. Vulnerable would be an understated way to describe how I felt.

Still, I had a motive for the evening other than exercise and I had to push aside my fear and get on with it. I waited till we were in the jaccuzi to talk. Partly it was my desire for more safety, but my delay was just as much for practical reasons. Saunas are poorly illuminated. I was going to have to carry of this conversation without signs. I can't lip read at all when I can't see well.

After congratulating him again on his victory I brought up what had been on my mind for hours.

"This is sort of awkward for me, but there's something I have to tell you. I know Aton is your friend but I saw him bring your mailing list to a copy center this morning. I'm a pretty good judge of facial expressions and he looked secretive, not like he was on an errand for you."

"He wasn't. Our mailing list is confidential. It's not supposed to leave the office."

"Then he's up to something."

"I thought so."

"What do you mean you *thought* so?"

"I've always been suspicious of him."

"In the office the other day you spoke as if the two of you were best buddies."

"That was just an act. I didn't know you then."

"What about the 'friendly competition' between the two of you for Sarah?"

"There was none. Sarah was working for me, under-cover, so to speak, trying to find out why he volunteered and what he was up to."

"I'll do the spying for you now," I said. It looked like I had my man. "Sarah can't and she was a friend of mine."

"Thanks. I'd like to catch the bastard at whatever he's doing." Up till then he'd been speaking coolly. Suddenly, like on the court, the ferocity came into his face. "I hate him," he said, "somehow he put a spell on Sarah. If it weren't for him Sarah and I would be together. I hope he gets what he deserves."

His rage was infectious. "Me too," I said. "I'll get him. I don't know how yet, but I'll figure out a way. I'll get him."

Rudy led the way back to Berkeley. He continued on to his place in San Francisco and I went to Nancy's. As heavily as my mind was in gear I'm lucky I arrived without mishap. It was hard to concentrate on driving.

It seemed I'd underestimated the effect Sarah had had on me. Tom, Rudy, Aton, Charlotte, and Nancy had all been profoundly influenced by her. I thought I "knew" her but apparently I'd been rash. I'd been so sure that jealousy was the motive. Sarah had been as beautiful a woman as there is in California or any other state. I know that makes other women jealous. She hadn't limited her affections to one man. I know that makes men jealous.

Then I learned that she'd been working as a spy. I had been blind to that possibility but as soon as Rudy told me I could visualize it clearly. I didn't need to ask him how he got her to do it. I could picture her outrage at the thought that Aton might be despoiling and violating the sanctity of the heliother-apy center. The plan might well have been her idea.

Apparently she'd found out something more significant than Aton's illicit photocopying. But she hadn't had the chance to tell Rudy what. The knowledge was buried with her. I had to uncover it without getting buried myself.

I thought back to a fortune that one of my students plucked out of his cookie during Chinese night at my school.

He knew all the words but hadn't been able to make heads-or-tails-or-edges out of it. "Don't trouble trouble," it read, "until trouble troubles you." It's good advice that many of my students ignore so I took pains to explain it to him clearly. It struck me on the drive from The Supreme Court to Nancy's that I was well on my way to ignoring that advice myself. And my plans called for nothing but getting in deeper.

Nancy was as ready, willing, and able as she had been the previous two nights but I wasn't. I was exhausted and the racquetball had been the least of it. I'd spent most of the day having mouth-to-mouth conversations. I can do it but it's a strain. I don't have to concentrate when I sign or watch signing but to lip read I do. Try wtching T.V. with the sound off if you want to get an idea what it's like. Or, you can trust me, it's not fun.

When I wasn't lip reading or knocking a ball or my body against walls I'd been doing that to my brain. So many mistakes. If they hadn't arrested the wrong man I'd have felt some sympathy for the police. Solving murders isn't easy—neither finding out who, nor collecting the evidence to prove it.

I was so exhausted that I honestly wanted to get into the same bed with Nancy and go straight to sleep. With a less determined woman I'm sure I would have succeeded. I won't give away her secret techniques. It's enough to say that she foiled my plan. She's a persuasive woman.

9

I had Nancy call Rudy early the next morning to have him join us for breakfast before they went to the office. I explained everything I'd found out. I needed help and they were as eager to catch Aton as I was. Rudy and Nancy had commitments other than the investigation so I would be the leader of the team. (I'd pushed my own commitments 3000 miles to the east to the furthest reaches of my mind.) I also felt that this was my "case." I'd take help whenever I needed it but this one was *mine*. Tom had called *me*.

My plan was to follow Aton. To see what he was doing I had to see what he was doing. Rudy said that Aton came to work via car so that's how I'd follow him. Rudy agreed to go to work first, find out where Aton was parked and what time he planned to leave, then call me through Nancy. After that she'd join Rudy at work as usual.

Rudy would check on a name to see if the original mailing list was back in the office but say nothing beyond that. What I'd seen was to remain a secret between the three of us. When I had something more solid I'd bring it to Jefferson and the police.

We agreed to meet back at Nancy's place but had to leave the time open. Who knew what I would see or how long I'd have to stay away. Nancy offered to convert her library into a "war room." Under my guidance it could be the central place to map strategies and coordinate action. Rudy and I liked the idea so her offer was accepted.

Rudy's call from a coffee shop near the heliotherapy center came only half an hour after he left us. The mailing list was back, Aton had parked on a side street, and was planning to leave at twelvish. Rudy advised me to be in position by 11:30. I said I'd be there by 11:00. If Aton seemed itchy before that, Rudy was to find some excuse to hold him. Nancy left as planned and I sat in the newly established headquarters to think.

What I thought about was assumptions. A month before I'd attended a professional development workshop for my normal job that stressed the importance of not making assumptions. The speaker cutely diagrammed how they make an ASSofUandME. He had numerous examples both humorous and serious.

On this case I'd been acquiring my own examples of mistaken assumptions but the issue is not that simple. Our lecturer had been warning us that what we take for granted may be wrong. It's important for a counselor or a detective to remember that. (It's a little easier to do when you sign since the base sign for "assume" is the same as the one for "guess.") However, life would be unmanageable if we had to act as if everything we depended on were unreliable.

Almost all canned food found in the supermarket is safe to eat, almost all drivers stop their cars at red lights. The day after it is 80° it is more than unlikely to snow. Yet, in all of those examples there is some degree of uncertainty.

To keep yourself both alive and sane you must find a balance. My whole trip to California was based on an assumption that people more knowledgeable about crime assumed was wrong—namely, that Tom was innocent. I knew I was right so I didn't clutter my mind testing the veracity or validity of that "fact."

I had also assumed jealousy to be the motive and that had been a mistake. I had to work hard, then, to keep my mind open to all possibilities. I had no time, therefore, to worry about poisoned food, drivers running stop lights, or an earthquake, even though scientists assume that to be a near certainty. The only question, they say, is when. If the "big one" came, my investigation, (and a lot more) would be disrupted whatever I did. I prefer to think of assumptions as risks. There are some you should avoid but some you have to take, and you can always reevaluate the odds.

I drove to the heliotherapy center's neighborhood and found Aton's car, a $12,000 Celica. Volunteers don't get paid and the last I heard Toyota was not giving away cars. I was interested to find out the source of his income. (The car could be stolen but he still needed to eat.) I parked under a tree several cars and a few hundred yards away and waited. The shade gave me some cover but was no guarantee.

It was only 45 minutes before I saw him but during that time I once again empathized with the police. I've read accounts of stakeouts lasting days. Mine was less than an hour but it was a hard fight against boredom. I had my *Hitchhiker's Guide. . .* with me but I'd brought it for appearance only. My eyes had to stay above the pages. If I yielded to the temptation to look at the print I would likely fail. Since I couldn't hear him approaching, I had to see him. Also, once into a good book I can get lost in another world (in this case many other worlds) and be gone for hours. I had to stay right there in Berkeley, California, alert and awake.

Aton strolled casually to his car, apparently not noticing me. He still looked dumpy but didn't seem concerned or worried. He pulled out and I followed a few seconds later. For that first block I had no choice but to be directly behind him. There were no other moving cars in the street. Once he turned on to Telegraph, however, I maintained a distance of one or two cars behind him. I felt two cars to be better for keeping me and my car out of his awareness but I also had to worry about getting caught at a light. (If I disrupted other drivers assumptions about red lights I could well cause an accident, involving me.)

The first part of his route was normal. From Telegraph he made a left on Ashby and took that all the way to 17 and thence to the Bay Bridge. He was headed for San Francisco. My first tailing problem came at the toll plaza. If I stayed behind him in the same lane he could easily shoot too far ahead after paying his fare, especially if he knew I was following but he'd shown no sign of that. I had to pick a nearby lane with the right speed of procession to let me pay only a second or two after him.

To my satisfaction I succeeded and we headed off to "the city." (Note the lower case letters. Suburbanites traveling to the nations capital say they're going to D.C. Re Chicago it's The Loop and for most other cities it's usually "downtown" or the city name or nickname. Only two cities are called, or call themselves, "the city" as if there is no other, no other city that could be your destination. San Francisco is one and the other is where I grew up.)

I don't know if you've seen Bullit or any of the episodes of The Streets of San Francisco. If you have, and can still remember parts of them, I'll lay 10-1 odds that what you remember are the car chase scenes. The streets are that steep and that hazardous to drive. So far this wasn't a chase, just a tail, but I didn't know how I'd react to a chase in San Francisco. I'm a good driver but have never been, nor intend to be, in a Grand Prix. Speeds over 75 make me nervous whether I'm driving or a passenger.

Fortunately I'd driven in San Francisco before and knew what I was up against. The inclines are hard on engines and the stop signs near the tops of hills are murder on transmissions but it's downhill that's scary. Cross streets interrupt the descent so you straighten out periodically, but for the first second of your redescent you can't see whatever might be in front of you. You can see the beautiful blue bay or a far off hill while your car is level but until you dip, the street in front of your hood and wheels is invisible. You take it slowly, but it's startling the first time you do it and part of that sensation always remains. You never become completely inured.

I kept my one or two car distance as Aton took the long exit ramp of the bridge onto Broadway and downtown. (Broadway is San Francisco's "sin center" but somehow feels laughable compared to New York's sordid and threatening 42nd St.) As

56

Aton continued I tried to make sense of his route. It almost felt like he was giving me a tour. We drove down to Fisherman's Wharf, up Nob Hill, then over to Golden Gate Park. The most logical destination from there would be the Golden Gate Bridge and Marin county and then who knows where but he certainly could have reached the Golden Gate more directly.

My first presentiment came when he turned on to Lombard Street and headed back downtown. (San Franciscan readers should know what's coming.) At that point Lombard is a major thoroughfare leading from the Golden Gate Bridge toward the center of the city. It's not as heavily trafficked as Market or Van Ness but it's a busy road. There are many businesses on each side including a motel row.

When Lombard crosses Van Ness, however, it changes dramatically. The flow of traffic bears right or left and Lombard starts going up, very steeply up. At that point I was two cars behind and knew what was going on. There was no way to pass as we climbed.

Lombard crests at Hyde. Before you start down there's a cute sign. Forgive my art, but it looks something like this: Yes, It's a warning for the crooked street. If you're one of the few people in the world who hasn't seen at least a postcard of it, go to any bookstore and look at any book with pictures of San Francisco. Then you'll know my sinking feeling.

I'd driven down the most crooked street in the world many times before but always for fun. On the preceding two blocks it had been virtually impossible for me to pass. Once Aton crossed Hyde two cars ahead of me and we started down it became literally impossible and I mean not even a fraction of a percent greater than zero. I could see him clearly but I knew that being even one car behind at that point would probably be too much. I don't know how long he'd been aware that I'd been following him, but there was no doubt about it then. He'd probably been playing with me for some time. I zigged and zagged at less than five miles an hour. So did he, but he was two fucking cars ahead. I felt humiliated, frustrated, and angry. Some detective I was.

And to top it all he stopped briefly at the end of the last zag. He stuck his head out of the window of his car, waved at me, then spun a fast right on Leavenworth. The two sightseers in front of me took their sweet time but even if I could have made them aware of the situation it wouldn't have mattered. The crooked street just doesn't permit speed. By the time I could straighten out Aton was long gone.

I've been angry before but I could only describe my feelings then as rage. That bastard. I have no god to swear to so I made an oath to myself that I would nail him. Tom may be psychologically and constitutionally unable to kill someone but I'm no longer so sure about myself. If I had had Aton in my hands at that moment vengance and anger may well have overcome all my reason. Pure and simple, I hated him. That murderous bastard.

10

I drove slowly back to Berkeley. What a wonderful plan I had concocted. What did it matter that we knew about Aton? He knew that we were on to him. We'd never see him again. The heliotherapy center had just lost a volunteer and I'd just lost my chance of freeing Tom.

I could tell Jefferson about the discrepancy of the missing bookend but would that be enough to find reasonable doubt? I wasn't hopeful. And what could I tell the police or Jefferson about Aton—that he'd waved at me? Sarah's spying and what I saw at the Kwique Coy Center would hardly get the police to pursue an unknown man. Between, Rudy, Nancy, and I, all we knew about him for sure was his physical appearance. His car and license number were possibles while his name was surely a fake. Only Sarah had known more and she was dead. Murdered.

But then I had an idea. I don't know how inspiration strikes me. I've woken up in the middle of the night with the words and/or signs I should have used with a student I'd counseled during the day. I have a tendency to think of the perfect thing to say to women just after they've turned their backs. I wrote the only poem I've ever had published during a boring college lecture.

My good idea about how to continue my investigation happened while I was passing a truck on my return trip across the Bay Bridge. I can't recall what the truck looked like but I can remember suddenly wondering why I hadn't searched another house. This case was making me feel very stupid very often.

59

Studying the scene of the crime is important. It answers "what," usually provides the key clues to "how," and sometimes "who." But people are murdered because of what happened when they were alive: what they did, how they lived, what they saw or heard or learned. Since my original theory seemed wrong I had to sit back and concentrate on "why." I couldn't get into Sarah's mind directly but there was a place I could look for clues—Sarah's house.

My search of Tom's apartment had told me how Tom lived and Sarah died. I needed to change my focus and find out more about how Sarah lived. To do that it made sense to re-see where she lived. I hadn't been there in over three years and the only things I could remember clearly were the cookbooks and the "jungleness."

I drove first to Jefferson's office. He wasn't in so I explained to his secretary what I needed. She typed a deputizing letter similar to the one I'd given to Sergeant Grimsley except that this time it was addressed to To-Whom-it-May-Concern. I knew that Sarah's landlord lived above her in the two-family house (even though both "families" were singles) but I'd never met him.

Sarah lived in the Elmwood section of Berkeley on Stuart Street. It's a slightly higher than middle class area. Palm trees are common and the neighborhood 7-11 sells The New York Times, daily as well as Sunday. When I worked at C.S.D. I frequented one of the local businesses, Sweet Dreams Candy and Ice Cream Parlor.

I was lucky to find Sarah's landlord home, but unlucky that he had both the time and desire to talk to me before he let me into Sarah's. His name is Woods Beach and is a professor at the university. He had a friendly smile and demeanor but the 300plus pounds on his 5′9″ frame were unsightly.

It wasn't his physique, however, that bothered me. It was his mind. He told me that he was nominally a professor of Psychology but in fact was an instructor and researcher in Parapsychology. He teaches three courses each semester: The History of Parapsychology, Theories of Parapsychology, and Research Methodology in Parapsychology.

60

I'm trying my best to keep an open mind about parapsychology (after all I do enjoy reading science fiction) but people like Woods Beach make it difficult. It wasn't that hard to put a mental "hold" on what he was teaching, but then he explained his research to me—and how I could help him. I was a perfect subject, he said, because I was deaf.

You see, his theory is that communicating with the dead is similar to communicating to the deaf. Instead of using interpreters you use "mediums." He pointed out to me how close the words "deaf" and "dead" were—just one letter different, (as if I hadn't known that for twenty years.)

The longer I stayed and payed attention to what he said or wrote (he often wanted to be sure he was making himself perfectly clear) the more I wanted to scream "Just give me the damn key and find some other dupe," but I couldn't risk alenating him. I had to see Sarah's. He said that the future of parapsychology research was in discovering the language of the dead.

"Do you think there's any parallel to sign language?" he asked me.

"No."

"Why not?"

I have a hard time knowing how to respond to idiocy except with sarcasm but I didn't want to seem snide in that situation. I wracked my brain for something to say.

"Because we're taught it by other people who are still alive," was the best I could do.

"That's a good point. I hadn't thought of that."

"I'd love to talk to you more about it. It's a fascinating topic, (I was pleased, if not proud, that I could say that without gagging.) but I can't concentrate on it properly now, while I'm trying to find Sarah's murderer. It wouldn't be fair to you for me to assist you in your work when my mind wasn't really in it. I'd be happy to come back and talk more after this is all over." (As I have noted before, I know how to lie.) "Can I have the key to Sarah's?"

"You will come back to see me later?"

"Scout's honor." (I dropped out before making Tender-foot.)

"Okay."

I fled down the stairs feeling lucky that I still had my mind. Ph.D. or not, Woods Beach certainly didn't have his. Only in Berkeley can such a man get paid for doing what he's doing.

Sarah was dead but most of her plants were still alive. Horticulture is one of my many areas of ignorance so I can't list the numerous variety of plants she had, but I could recognize some cacti and ferns. The cookbooks were in the kitchen where I'd seen them last as were the self-help books in the bedroom. Both collections had grown considerably.

I didn't pay much attention to the plants or the books. I was looking for an unknown something that I didn't already know. What that sentence means is that I didn't know what I was looking for but that her books and plants were old news. I wanted new news, something connected with her unnaturally shortened career as a spy.

I searched her apartment as thoroughly as I scoured Tom's for the unrealized bookend. I didn't have a policewoman watching me but Woods Beach lived above. Of the two presences, Sergeant Grimsley was far and away the one I preferred.

I found nothing, so I searched again. It was quite possible that there was nothing to be found, but that thought was too distressing to contemplate. I had to give it another try. The second search revealed nothing new but I saw one small thing in different way.

On Sarah's desk was her current Sierra Club Wilderness Engagement Calendar. Their calendars are justly famous for their pictures. I couldn't help but marvel at some of the photographs as I flipped through it.

When I'd looked at it the first time I'd noticed that Sarah hadn't listed any of her engagements in the slots provided, which were the reverse sides of the pictures. I supposed she hadn't wanted to mar even the backs of those representations of the beauty in nature. What I wanted, however, was at the end, in the section for addresses.

Tom's address was there, as was Rudy's, but Nancy's wasn't. (Why not?) There were several others, both men and women whose names I didn't recognize. Of course there was no listing for an "Aton" either as a first or last name. I planned to take the book with me and show it to Tom to see what he knew about the other names when I realized that I probably didn't have to.

I don't know what your address book looks like but mine is near chaos. For every name and phone number I've entered under the proper call letter I have a dozen that are not. They're not in the wrong place as much as they're no place. I've just stuck them under the cover on index cards, backs of envelopes, bits of napkins, etc. wherever the people I've met have written them down for me. (I even have one on a scrap of toilet paper but that's another story.) Cleaning out my book is always on my list of chores to be done but only gets accomplished twice a decade or so.

Sarah's was very unlike mine. All her addresses were properly entered in alphabetical order with blanks between most so she could make additions without upsetting the alphabet. Wondrous, amazing. But there was one unentered address and phone number just stuck in like one of mine. It was on the back of a recipe card for Chocolate Chip Quiche. Perhaps she considered the vital information as unreal as the recipe because it was for one "John Smith." Mr. "Smith" lived on Ashbury Street in San Francisco, near Haight.

I had very little doubt that John Smith was an alias and that John Smith went by at least one other alias—namely Aton. I took the whole book with me when I left but that was just precautionary. I also kept the key and didn't go back upstairs to talk with Woods, then or ever.

I arrived home before Nancy so I thought I'd take advantage of that time to do some work while I ate. I went to the McDonald's that Tom had recently been working for. I actually find Chicken McNuggets with sweet and sour sauce to be tasty, if not gourmet. And, of course, they don't rank with Burritos, Eclairs, or Ice Cream.

I got my McNuggets but no useful information. A McDonald's is a McDonald's. They look the same and the food is the same, by design. I asked one of the workers about Tom. He said that Tom was too nice a boss, (he could be taken advantage of), but that no one at the restaurant knew him well personally. The first thing they heard about his non-work life was his arrest. They were sure he didn't do it but no one knew anything to help.

Nancy still wasn't home when I got back so I settled down with my *Hitchhikers Guide*. . . . I had just finished when she arrived around 11:00. I promised her an interesting account of my eventful day but asked her to make two calls for me first. She complied.

The first call was to Rudy, setting up another breakfast war council for the next day. The second was to be a wrong number. I told her to disguise her voice (There are times I wish I could disguise my signs but the face is part of sign language so that's difficult.) and ask for Abigail or Ezekial or some other nonentity. I wanted just one piece of information and I got it. She did recognize the voice that had answered and said "hello." Her friend and mine—Aton.

After that I started to describe my day but I could see that she didn't want to hear it. To tell the truth, I didn't want to either. Lombard Street and Woods Beach, though memorable, had not been enjoyable.

Oddly enough, Nancy and I could read each other's minds. Woods Beach might call it telepathy, but I don't. Mutual lust would be a better phrase. A good book can help me forget my problems, but a good woman and a waterbed are even better.

11

Planning and food seem to go together. At my school, the bigger the big shots who are meeting or the more significant the topic the more likely there is to be pastries and coffee. There are times I wonder if the food helps or hinders my administrators thought processes, but Nancy's omelets and coffee seemed to help the three of us reach agreement quickly. Catching Aton was to be our top priority. Rudy would close the heliotherapy center for the day and appropriate some funds to cover whatever expenses (within reason) that we might incur. We wouldn't alert the police yet because we had nothing solid to tell them.

It was hard to believe, but it had not even been a week since the murder. Our war council was meeting on a Friday morning. Sarah had been killed the previous Friday night. I had only been in California since Sunday. More had happened to me in those few days than in any other similar span of time. (Little did I know then how much more was to come.) I hoped to finish everything by the end of the weekend. If not, I'd have to make an unpleasant phone call to my boss. He's deaf, like me, but he only wants to pay me when I show up to work. (How unreasonable of him.) Oh well, that was a bridge I'd have to cross if and when I came to it.

As we sat and discussed what to do I came to a realization about our team. We had just about everything we should need to face the unexpected: eyes, ears, brains, brawn, beauty, etc. but we were missing one very important element for this particular job. Aton knew all of us. He could recognize all of us by sight. He might not know that Rudy and Nancy had joined me but I didn't want to rely on that. He knew I was after him. If he were a careful criminal he would assume that we would join forces. If he espied any of us in Haight-Ashbury or any other unlikely place he'd be able to put two and two together.

What our team needed, therefore, was someone Aton didn't know. That person also had to be someone we could trust. Who knew what situations we might run up against. We needed someone who had the motivation to help us—for free. This was our business, Sarah and/or the heliotherapy center had been important to us. Even if we wanted a professional private detective we couldn't have afforded one.

I was able to think of someone that fit the bill but it was not a pleasant thought. I have my pride. I don't like to swallow it but I didn't see where I had much choice. To enlist who I had in mind I'd be certain to suffer some indignities. I made a mental note to present to Tom, when this whole thing was over, a bill for many many burritos.

Nancy and Rudy saw my point and agreed to accept responsibility for the watch over Aton till I got back with our new teammate. Rudy took the first shift while Nancy left to get the equipment. Once again I drove south to Fremont and the new C.S.D.

Charlotte was not pleased that I interrupted her lunch. "What the hell are you doing here?"

"I came to see you."

"What makes you think that I want to see you?"

"Nothing. Don't get the idea that I'm here on a social call. If I didn't need you to help me catch Sarah's murderer and free Tom I wouldn't be here."

"What can a mere woman like me do to help the wonderful super-hero deaf detective."

I came close, very close, to saying *Shut up and listen*, but exercised some restraint. "I know who did it, but he knows I'm after him. There are two others on the team but he knows them too. We have to have an unknown."

"And I'm your unknown?"

66

"Yes."

"Forget it."

"I thought you wanted Tom out of jail."

"I do, but I have no desire to go off on some wild goose chase just because of your inflated ego. If you know who did it, tell the police and let them do their job. Or haven't you thought of something so simple."

"I don't have anything to tell them, or at least nothing they'd believe."

"And I'm supposed to believe you?"

"Listen to what I have to say and then decide. Make an effort to judge what I say and not let our quite mutual dislike color your judgement."

"Go ahead. I'm curious to hear what this non-evidence is."

I explained carefully. I told her about the missing bookend, the unauthorized photocopying, and Sarah's short career as a spy. I didn't want to, but I also relived my humiliation on Lombard St. I could see her gloat as I told it, but I think that that was what convinced her.

"I wish I'd been there to see your face," she said.

"That's not an answer. Will you help or not? I'll promise to try to be civil."

"That's quite a concession. With that understanding I'll help and make the same promise."

"Fine. Since time is of the essence I'd suggest that you develop a sudden migraine and let your principal know that you have to go home early."

"I think I can do that."

"Fine. I'll follow you to your place while you pack an overnight bag. I don't know where this chase may lead us."

"I'll pack a bag but you're not following me no place. I know how to drive to Berkeley all by myself. Just tell me where and give me about half an hour here to take care of my own business."

"Okay." I gave her Nancy's address.

"*Nancy* Kramer," she said. "I see I was right the other day about the 'person' you were staying with."

"I thought we were trying to be civil?"

"Sorry, I forgot."

Nancy enjoyed meeting Charlotte. It gave her a chance to use sign language with someone other than me. She was pleased to see that they could understand each other. Charlotte seemed to be using her voice (she was moving her lips) but I had no way to tell how understandable her speech was without asking someone.

"The last time I saw you was when you came to the heliotherapy center," Nancy said, "and argued with Sarah. I didn't understand anything."

"I could still sign so that you couldn't understand me, if I wanted to, but I have nothing to say to him, (wonderfully tactful Charlotte pointed to me) that I'm afraid for you to know."

"We're a team, remember," I said. "It's time we left the war room and joined Rudy on the battle front."

"Okay."

"Okay."

The three of us rode together in Charlotte's Le Car to the health food cafe in Haight-Ashbury to meet Rudy. Like Charlotte, her car would be an unknown to "Mr. Smith." On the way Nancy donned the wig I asked her to purchase and put some women's paint on her face. She wouldn't fool Aton close up but that wasn't the purpose of the disguise. From a distance or through a rear view mirror, accompanied by another woman, I doubted he'd spot her.

The cafe was across from Aton's building, a victorian town house at an angle of 75 degrees. Rudy was sitting at a window table. He could see Aton's entrance clearly but the lighting and position made it highly unlikely that Aton could see him, even if Aton looked in the right place.

We joined him, I introduced Charlotte, and we got down to business.

"If he's left the building," Rudy said, "he did it before I got here."

Simultaneously, Nancy and I found ourselves interpreting for Charlotte but our assistance was not appreciated.

"You're not the only person who can lip read, you know," Charlotte said to me.

To Nancy, she was more polite. "Thank you for wanting to help, but I'd prefer not to depend on you. Keep signing when *you* talk but I'll try to lip read Rudy. If I don't understand I'll ask you to tell me what I missed. Okay?"

"Fine," said Nancy.

We split up into teams, by sex, but not for reasons connected to sex. One hearing person needed to be in each group to use the walkie-talkies that Nancy just bought. The other possible mixed combination was Nancy-and-I and Rudy-and-Charlotte. Communication could be vital and despite Charlotte's protestations that she could lip read (all of "us" can to some degree or other) I trusted my own ability more, especially now that I knew Rudy and his lip and facial movements. Another factor was that the two cars we had with us were Rudy's and Charlotte's. The driving could turn out to be crucial too and people are generally better at driving their own cars than they are strangers' cars. And if there were to be a chase I wanted Rudy's MGB and my generalship involved in the primary chase car.

Rudy and I stayed in the cafe till the women went to their car and got in position. Next, we left and went to Rudy's car to wait. While we waited and watched I dined on a piece of carrot cake I'd bought to take out and we talked about the neighborhood we were in, Haight-Ashbury, and its evolution. In the Sixties it was the renowned symbol of the counter-culture—flower power, flower children alternate life-styles, and a rejection of the materialism and militarism of the world at large.

The peace movement faded more slowly in Haight-Ashbury than in the rest of the U.S., but fade it did. Sadly, only the worst part of the counter-culture remained. In the Seventies Haight-Ashbury became a haven for drugs, and not the peaceful pot of love-ins but the dangerous dope of addiction and crime. Haight Street became unsafe to walk at night.

The Eighties, however, seemed to be bringing a revival, though not a recreaction of the old. The druggies were mostly gone, being pushed out by the crunch of the San Francisco housing market. A diverse group of blacks, whites, latins, and gays were buying, refurbishing, and renovating houses. The common denominator for the new settlers was money. The cost of buying or renting in San Francisco is second in the nation, trailing only (you guessed it) Manhattan. Haight-Ashbury was becoming gentrified.

I wondered again about Aton. Where did he get the money to live here? What kind of gentry was he?

It was a long wasted afternoon. Either Aton had fled early in the morning or he had stayed inside all day. As dusk approached we left our position for a short time since the women were also in position to see the front door. (I wondered how they were getting along.) Rudy and I drove around the block and first determined that the only other exit from Aton's building was a fire-escape ladder.

Next we drove around the neighborhood looking for Aton's car. If it was gone and he'd escaped us early or via the ladder we were in trouble, but we found the car on Clayton. Hopefully that meant he was still inside. Why hadn't I thought of looking for the car earlier. It would have saved us a lot of worry. Another lesson learned in my crash course in crime detection and solution. We took up a position at the opposite end of the block from his car and radioed our action to the women.

It was a long and wasted night too. At nine we sent Nancy and Charlotte to Rudy's apartment to get some sleep. Rudy lived on Bay, near Fisherman's Wharf, within the five mile range of the walkie-talkies. At three in the morning they came back and relieved us. I was curious to see Rudy's place but it was dark and I was exhausted. After he opened the sofa bed for me I conked out and slept soundly.

I was startled when he tapped me on the shoulder to rouse me. We'd only allotted ourselves 5½ hours sleep so I was pulled from some long since forgotten dream, but his tap was doubly unsettling. I'm used to waking to my alarm (It flashes a light in my face.) so the shoulder tap that is a standard way of getting a deaf person's attention was, in that situation, a reminder to me of how awkward a position I was in.

After toiletting and a fast cup of coffee we went back to work. We stopped at a 7-11 for some donuts for ourselves and the women then completed the rendezvous at 9:00. There was no talk about how long we would have to keep up the stakeout. We were determined to see it through.

We took the position on Aton's block and had Nancy and Charlotte watch his car. Mercifully, it was only half an hour before we were able to radio good (?) news. Aton had left his domicile and was casually walking in the direction of his car.

At 9:45 that Saturday morning Rudy's MGB, with the two of us in it, was the last car in a three car caravan across the Golden Gate Bridge. We were out of sight of the other two, but not out of contact.

12

There are many roads you can travel again and again and never really see them. Your eyes are open and you notice what's around you but nothing makes a lasting impression. You're hard pressed to remember details. California's Rte. #1 is not one of those roads.

It has been said that there is a correlation (causation?) between beauty and danger. My father has often warned me to avoid beautiful women, citing the maxim "All that glitters is not gold." His ensuing advice is to court plain or homely women and he quotes Tolkien's revision "All that is gold does not glitter."* I don't know about women in general, but with Sarah there was at least a connection between beauty and disaster.

In regard to Rte. 1 beauty and danger go hand in hand. They are interwoven and inseperable. It's name is the Pacific Coast Highway and it follows the coast, even when the coast is mountain cliffs. The road often twists and turns, on the cliffs, thousands of feet above the sea. There's just enough room for one lane of traffic in each direction. A small miscalculation to the right and swerve off the road by a northbound driver will send the car against the face of the mountain. A similar slip by a southbound driver can send the car plunging to the ocean or beach far far away. (California doesn't believe in guard rails since they spoil the natural beauty of the landscape.)

Aton was leading the cavalcade up Rte. 1. The times I'd been on it before I'd been the driver. Even with one's attention

---

*The Fellowship of the Ring p. 325.

73

thusly limited it's a spectacular sight. With Rudy driving I could turn my head and look all around. There's a stretch north of San Francisco where the road winds through redwood trees that are an offshoot of Muir Woods before it reaches the cliffs. I usually prefer noticing fauna to flora but redwoods are worth seeing. Tall, towering, and wide, they're majestic.

The women reported to Rudy on the "phone" that they were having no trouble following Aton. Of course, for much of the way there'd be no place for him to turn off, unless he were suicidal. They were three cars behind him and after the woods, could see him clearly. He'd certainly have seen their car but following in line is the order of the day on the Pacific Coast Highway so it seemed unlikely that he suspected them of doing any more than following the dictates of the road.

Rudy was driving faster than I would have been comfortable doing but he seemed to corner each turn smoothly so I kept my mouth shut—until the first crack. Rudy said that Nancy had warned him about the cracks but I consider Nancy to have made a classic understatement. When we reached the first one all the cars ahead of us slowed to near zero. Rudy took it at under five miles per hour but I still almost hit the roof (literally.)

The "cracks" were actually a shift in the very fabric of the mountain, downward, caused by the rain, rain, and more rain that California had had for months before I arrived. (Nancy had thanked me for bringing the miraculous relief. I accepted the credit with "You're welcome" but I don't think she took me seriously.) I'd seen pictures in the newspapers of the mud slides closing parts of Rte. 1 south of San Francisco. Here, north of San Francisco, a different phenomenon had occured. The earth above the road hadn't fallen to any appreciable degree. Instead, in places the western half of the road, the side closest to the cliff, had sunk several inches forming mini-cliffs for cars to traverse.

Rudy did slow down after the jolt of that first one and never came close to losing control of the car but my fear was something more ominous. Despite what I wrote earlier, for the first time since I'd been in California I worried about an earthquake. Rain alone had almost destroyed the road and left it battered. The cracks made me realize how easily and suddenly this road could disappear. In its vulnerable state it wouldn't require the "big one" either. A relatively minor tremblor, with an epicenter at what would otherwise be a safe distance, would do the job quite nicely. I like to swim, but had no desire to reach the beach via free fall.

Yes, Rte. 1 is beautiful; yes, Rte. 1 is dangerous. I'll probably drive it again when I'm not chasing a murder suspect. To me, beauty is a temptation.

We were past the cliffs and were near Inverness and Point Reyes when the women radioed that Aton had turned off onto a private drive. We told them to keep a watch on the entrance and wait for us. We rendezvoused five minutes later and I saw the triangular wooden sign at the front of the narrow lane. From Rte. 1 there was no view, or clue to the final destination of the lane except for the information on the sign.

The small letters near the bottom read: Visitors Welcome, Please Register at the Office. I decided to take up the offer because of the larger letters. There wasn't a cloud in the sky and the sun was directly overhead; I could read them clearly. Aton had led us to THE UNIVERSITY OF THE SUN.

It was time to discuss tactics since I didn't want to go in when Aton was there. I wanted to know as much as I could about the University of the Sun without his knowing about my visit. Fortunately there was a restaurant on the highway within view of the entrance—Viktor's Hungarian Restaurant. I'd never had Hungarian food before but when it comes to food I'm a willing gambler.

Viktor's wasn't crowded (perhaps it drew a big dinner business) so we didn't have to wait for a table by the front window. We needed to watch as we brunched. I chose Viktor's Goulash, Rudy had Viktor's Pot Pie, and both Nancy and Charlotte picked Viktor's Chicken. (There was no choice but to pick Viktor's something or other.) The back of the menu was a biography of Viktor including a description of his harrowing escape from the Cossacks and eventual emigration to America. Mrs.

Viktor and Viktor junior worked in the kitchen. Viktor waited on his customers personally.

When Viktor learned that Charlotte and I were deaf he offered us our meals for free but we both declined. The food would taste the same to us as it would to Rudy and Nancy, (I'll accept half-price for a movie since I can't hear the dialog, but I prefer to pay full fare to see foreign films since the subtitles let me follow the plot.)

All four of us were curious to see the University of the Sun but Aton still needed watching. Whenever he left the U. of S. where would he go? Home to Haight-Ashbury or to some place even stranger yet? Nancy and Charlotte weren't happy with the assignment of continuing to follow Aton but the same reasons we made them the car in his sight were still sound, so they acquiesced. We promised them a full recounting of what we saw at the "University". I played up the possibility that they might see something even more remarkable than us but I doubted it.

Viktor's Goulash was good and my companions enjoyed their vittles too. We all had time to finish the main course but not the coffee or dessert before the tell-tale Celica made its appearance and headed down Rte. 1 south toward San Francisco. Nancy and Charlotte had to dash out to be sure not to lose Aton, but Rudy and I took our time and finished dessert before embarking on our part of the adventure. Viktor was puzzled and upset that the women left without saying goodby. Rudy and I were upset that we got stuck with the whole bill, but that was the price we paid for taking the juicy assignment.

The entrance to the University of the Sun resembled that of a more famous institute of higher learning in the San Francisco Bay area. It was a narrower and shorter version of Palm Row at Stanford. I wondered if the mimicry was deliberate. I doubted that there would be much else in common between the two institutions. I was right.

The lane led to a Visitor's Center that was made of adobe (the sun-dried bricks made famous by the Peublos of the South-west) and had a thatch roof. Inside, however, modern civilization intruded via the presence of filing cabinets, electric lights, a typewriter, and a phone. There were two Amazons (They didn't say that but both women were over 6'2", tan, and well muscled.) sitting at two desks behind name plates that read, respectively, Tut, and Sphinx.

"Hi," I said to either of them. "We're prospective students and would like some information and a tour."

That's what we're here for," said Tut. "Follow us."

We complied. The main part of the "university" had been invisible from the small parking area and visitor's center. The view was blocked by a large hill that we had to walk around. Once the central "campus" came into view I knew that the placement had not been accidental. There were only two buildings, one completed, the other still under construction. Their size was impressive but I doubted that the university wanted them in view of the main road. They were both brick pyramids— scaled down replicas of the ancient Egyptian pyramids at Giza.

Too much sun can make you dizzy and light headed. Even more can fry you. I hadn't been basking or purposely catching rays, but I was getting my fill of this California preoccupation with the sun—heliotherapy, adobe, pyramids, etc. I didn't feel that I was light headed but that too many people around me were. (Canadians joke about their four seasons— June, July, August, and Winter—yet they seem to be a sane people.) The concrete of my Manhattan upbringing was beginning to seem sensible in comparison.

Rudy turned and whispered something to me. (I can't hear voices drop, but I can read furtive gestures.) "Oh no, not ? ? ?"

"What?"

"Later."

Flanked by Tut and Sphinx we entered the completed pyramid. We followed a corridor to a room that looked like a library: book shelves, reading tables, and students reading.

"This is our library," said Tut. "First stop on the tour. The entire university is contained within the walls of this pyramid, until the second one is completed. Students live and study here. The sun is the source of all energy (I'd heard that before.) but pyramids magnify and enhance it. Working here adds vitality to our life forces."

"What do you study?" Rudy asked.

"The eternal mysteries," said Tut.

"Like, 'Why is there a California?'" I retorted.

"Something like that," said Tut. In her smile and deflection of my sarcasm was a hint of seduction but I doubted it was an effort to bed me. I sensed more of an effort to recruit a new student.

"I see books," I said directly to Sphinx. "Why not papyrus?"

"As you can see," Tut answered, "we are not philosophically opposed to modern technology when it serves our needs. You should have noted our use of electricity."

"Are you deaf, like me?" I asked Sphinx, adding signs to my voice.

"No," said Tut, seemingly unfazed by my revelation. "Let me now show you our room. It is a typical one. We are students too."

"Why doesn't Sphinx speak?" I asked.

"She chooses not to."

Tut led the way out and down another brick corridor. Eternal mysteries. Like Sphinx? I wanted to study her. She was the taller of the two women, about 6'4" and her facial features more classically beautiful. Her silence was alluring. As I said, I find beauty tempting. But first things first. I had another mystery to solve and it was a very modern one.

Their room was sparse. Desks, flourescent lamps, sleeping pallets, and two small wooden wardrobes were the only furnishings. The only "decorations" were books on book shelves. There were other rooms along the corridor with a men's room at one end and a women's room at the other. Some student rooms were occupied by two women, some by two men, and some were coed. All rooms were doubles.

"Are there any rules for students," I asked.

"Only two," Tut answered. "No student may disturb the meditation or work of another, and no unnatural substances can be brought into the university."

"Are students free to come and go whenever they choose?" Rudy asked.

"Of course," Tut said.

"Give me an example of an unnatural substance," I said.

"Chicken McNuggets."

Next we were shown a classroom. It looked like a smaller version of the library: books around the walls and a wooden table with chairs in the center. As in the library and in Tut and Sphinx's room, I didn't recognize any of the books. As much as I read, I'm not up to date on the eternal mysteries.

Last stop was the cafeteria. As I expected, students at the University of the Sun ate only "natural" food. (Why is it that you rarely hear about the 100% natural plants that aren't so good to eat. For example—belladonna.*) Also, as expected, diet was an important part of the "curriculum." Besides the basics, student meals were supplemented by Spirulina. I'd never seen it before but Rudy said that health food stores in Berkeley sell several brands. It is a vitamin made from dried algae. Spirulina, Tut explained, not only absorbs sunlight but traps and stores it in a way that it becomes potentized. (I had to ask Tut to repeat that word twice before I understood it.) She offered some to us. Rudy tried one and said it tasted okay but I wouldn't touch the stuff. The tablets were dark green. Normally, I like to look at green plants, not eat them, but I don't even like the look of seaweed.

Before I record the final question and answer period with Tut I want to flash forward a little to the time when Rudy and I were finished with our tour, on our way out, and walking

---

*Interesting but irrelevant fact. In Italian, a "belladonna" isn't a deadly poison, but a beautiful woman. Ambrose Bierce avers that this shows how similar the English and Italian languages are.

toward his car, without the intimidating presence of Tut and Sphinx. I asked him about the word I'd missed when he'd whispered to me then put me off with "Later." He tried telling me, but no matter how many times he repeated it, I didn't catch it so we had to wait till we got to the car so he could find paper and pen to write it for me.

When he did, I understood the reason for my failure. Not only had I never seen the word on the lips before, I'd never seen it in print either and I doubt it's in the O.E.D.*—PYR-AMIDIOTS. He then wrote down its corollary, PYRAMIDIOCY. I love those two words but Rudy hates them. My viewpoint is that of a bibliophile and word freak. Rudy explained that it's pyramidiots and pyramidiocy that make it hard to convince people of the benefits of heliotherapy.

That may sound ridiculous, but to Rudy it was serious. He said that he was tired of people lumping and dumping them together. Whereas I was skeptical about the students at the University of the Sun, all of whom seemed to be Caucasians in their early twenties, Rudy saw them as heretics.

Back to the cafeteria with Tut and Sphinx.

"Who is building the second pyramid?" Rudy asked.

"Students," Tut answered. "We currently have a waiting list because we don't have room for all those who want to enroll. The new structure should alleviate the situation."

"Do they get paid?" he asked.

"It's part of the curriculum."

"You didn't answer his question," I said. "Do they get paid?"

"Not monetarily. They earn curriculum credits."

"How convenient," I said. "What's the tuition at the University of the Sun?"

"That depends. We have a sliding scale. It's based on ability to pay. No prospective student is ever turned down for financial reasons."

---

*13 Volume Oxford English Dictionary

"What would be the average tuition, and room and board, for a year, then?"

"I'm sorry, I can't answer that. That's confidential between the university and each student."

"I see," I said. "What about faculty. I didn't see any."

"Yes you did, you just didn't notice them since they look just like students. In fact they are only advanced students like Sphinx and myself, who have reached a level of awareness in certain areas that we are competent to share it with others."

"I assume," I said, "that the amount of faculty compensation is also confidential."

"You assume correctly."

"I have a different question," Rudy said. "Perhaps you can help me. I'm looking for a friend of mine. I think he may be a student here. He's about 5'3", has short black hair, and goes by the name of Aton."

"He's not a student," Tut replied. "He's the founder and chancellor."

"Oh," I said.

"When you see him," said Rudy, "give him my best. My name is Rudolph Alexis."

"I'll be sure to do that," said Tut.

13

It was dusk when our visit to the University of the Sun was over. I planned to come back again for an unannounced visit when there was no sunlight at all, but for the time being, Rudy and I were through. Without the sunlight we didn't return on Route 1; at night it isn't spectacular, just dangerous. There is a longer but safer drive through the towns of Marin so we took that.

We'd had to be vague about the rendezvous with the women. Nancy's apartment was to be the place but no time had been set. If Aton went back to his home in Haight-Ashbury, we told Nancy and Charlotte to go home. If he went somewhere else we wanted to know where but I felt reasonably sure that the key to the mystery lay somewhere in the University of the Sun.

I felt good about the day. It had been a productive one. I had more to learn but I felt a sense of accomplishment, that I was on the way to a resolution of the case. I asked Rudy to drive me to Nancy's. If they weren't there he was to go home and show up the next morning. If they were there we'd share information and plan.

It was quite dark when we arrived and Rudy pulled the car to a stop at the curb. I was getting out of the car when I felt a few things happen in rapid succession. Inexplicably, at the time, Rudy's hand slammed into my shoulder sending me sprawling toward the sidewalk, there was a searing pain in my head like I was being sliced with a knife, then my face rushed up to meet the sidewalk. It was a long time before I felt anything more.

When I awoke my head throbbed and my vision was blurry. After a few minutes I could see clearly but the headache hadn't abated. The first thing I noticed were the unmistakeable white walls. Add to that the sterile smell of the air and I knew where I was—a hospital. The shades were pulled over the windows but from the amount of light filtering through the cracks I judged it to be sometime in the morning.

I was in a semi-private room. The patient in the neighboring bed looked in worse shape than me. I tested all my limbs and though stiff, they all moved the way I asked them to. Except for the headache and some cuts on my face and head, I was okay.

My roommate was turning in pain. He seemed to be in a restless, comfortless, half-sleep. His left shoulder was heavily bandaged and in a sling. Whatever had hit me had hit him worse; my roommate was Rudy.

I could only guess what had happened, but as I found out later, my guess wasn't far wrong. Nature was calling me urgently and I found that I was able to rise and go to the bathroom by myself. If I could only ignore my throbbing head I'd feel fine.

As I was walking back to the bed a nurse came in and said something to me. I couldn't be sure but it looked like the profound observation "Oh, you're awake." (Headaches don't facilitate lip reading.) I was too tired and sore to answer quickly. It wouldn't have mattered anyway since right after she spoke the nurse turned and walked back through the door. I wanted to talk to Rudy to find out more about what had happened but I didn't want to disturb him. Sooner or later I'd find out and his semi-sleep was more important. If what I guessed was accurate, I owed him far more than I could ever repay.

I got back in bed to sleep, if I could, or, if not, just rest. I doubted I could have slept since my mind was churning so fast but Nancy's barging into the room five minutes later made the question academic. Her hug hurt but felt good anyway.

"Oh, Bob," thank God you're alive."

I felt like saying *Do you mean thank Rudy?* but it didn't seem to be the time to debate theology so I responded with a question. "What happened?"

"Someone took a shot at you."

"One shot? Just at me?"

"It's not clear. All I know is that I was sitting in my apartment reading when I hear Rudy scream 'Look out,' then a gunshot. Charlotte had dropped me off and gone back to Fremont. We'd followed Aton to San Francisco. He'd gone straight home. I was waiting for you when I heard everything."

"Where's Charlotte now?"

"In the waiting room. I've been here all night so the nurses promised to let me in when you woke up."

"How'd Charlotte know to come here?"

"After you were asleep for the night I called my neighbor and had him pin a note on my door for her."

"I see. What time is it?"

"About 11:00."

"Sunday morning?"

"Yes."

"How's Rudy."

"He'll be okay. He has a fractured collar bone from where the bullet struck him. The doctors got it out and it will mend. You were hit by the broken glass and got a concussion when you hit the sidewalk."

"So Rudy's shoulder took the bullet meant for my head?"

"Why do you say that?"

"Because he shoved me to the ground. He must have heard something, that I couldn't, to warn him."

"He didn't say anything about that but he was in a lot of pain. He didn't say much of anything."

"How did we get to the hospital?"

"I screamed for someone to call the police and ambulance."

"So the police know what happened."

"Yes."

"What do they know about our adventures of yesterday?"

"Nothing yet."

"Fine. Please don't tell them. Just stick to what happened outside your place. I'll tell them about our friend Mr. Smith, except for the visit to the University of the Sun. I want to keep that quiet for now."

"Okay. I'll go out and tell Charlotte too. The police should be on their way. I heard the nurse calling them."

Nancy left and though I hated to do it, I woke up Rudy. He tried to pretend that he hadn't been sleeping and that he was okay but since he hadn't known that Nancy had been in the room he was obviously being polite or macho, or both. He had been asleep and he was in pain. Fortunately I had just finished telling him about my conversation with Nancy, including my decision to keep quiet about the University of the Sun, when Sergeant Grimsley walked in.

"Good morning Mr. Brewer, Mr. Alexis."

"Good?" I said.

"<u>? ? ?</u>"

"Sergeant Grimsley, would you mind if Ms. Kramer came in to interpret for me. I can't lip read very well now. I'm hardly awake and my head is killing me."

"That should be all right." She left and came back in a minute with both Nancy and Charlotte. Nancy stood next to the sergeant, so I could see both clearly, and Charlotte took a chair and sat between my bed and Rudy's.

"My first question is to both Mr. Brewer and Mr. Alexis. Did you see who shot you?"

"I didn't," I said.

"Neither did I," Rudy said, "at least not clearly. I heard a rustling in the bushes. When I looked that way I saw a gun. I screamed 'Look out' but Bob couldn't hear me so I dove into him rather than try to see more."

"That was wise, seeing as you're both alive now. Do you have any idea who would want to kill you?"

Rudy and I looked at each other. He gave me a nod to go ahead. "Yes," I said, "but we don't know much about him.

86

As you know, I disagree with your department's conclusion about who murdered Sarah Collins a week ago. The man I suspect killed her was probably the same person who shot at us."

"Who is this man."

"Rudy knows the most."

"Mr. Alexis."

Rudy told her most of what he knew about Aton: his volunteer work, the suspected abuse of the mailing list, that Sarah had been trying to find out more, and his San Francisco address.

"Before we knew his address," I added, "I followed him by car to try to learn it, but he saw me and lost me on Lombard Street. Yesterday Rudy and I tried to follow him from his home but he lost us, this time on the Golden Gate Bridge."

Rudy's, Charlotte's, and Nancy's silence was a tacit approval of my lie.

"I will pay a visit to this mysterious Mr. Smith," said Sergeant Grimsley. "I will keep in mind your suspicion regarding the Sarah Collins case but I expect that from now on you leave police work to the police."

"I would never do anything to interfere," I said.

"Let's hope not. Ms. Grafton, Ms. Kramer, do you have anything to add?"

Charlotte said no and Nancy repeated what she told me about hearing the scream and the shot and rushing to the street and finding us.

"That's all for now then," the sergeant said, "but I'll be seeing you all again. Thank you for your cooperation."

After Sergeant Grimsley left Charlotte spoke up. "So what now?"

"We'll let the police do their job, as suggested," I said, "but I intend to pay another visit to the University of the Sun tonight."

"Tonight?" said Nancy. "The doctor said you were both supposed to stay here for a few days of observation."

"I have my own observation to do and I don't like hospitals. I don't know about Rudy, but I'll be out of here within the hour."

"If I can walk," he said, "I'm going with you." He slid out of bed and found that it hurt his shoulder each time he put his foot down but that his legs were fine. "You have a partner," he said.

"For our escape from here, fine, but not for tonight. Two people are more likely to be seen than one."

"You said what you were going to do," Charlotte said, but what about us?"

"You're off duty for now, but I do have some work for Rudy and Nancy."

"Why them and not me?"

"Sorry darling, but it's phone work and you're deaf, remember."

For an answer, all I got was a glare.

I explained what I wanted Rudy and Nancy to do. Rudy said he'd go to the office and start right away but Nancy was not so cooperative.

"I'll be happy to join Rudy later but first I'm taking you home. You are hurt and if you're going out tonight you need some rest now and I intend to see to it."

Charlotte was about to say something but I glared her silent. She left in a sulk after saying that she'd be back at Nancy's Monday after she finished teaching. Nancy watched for the nurses while Rudy and I found and donned our street clothes. Nancy popped back in and gave us the all clear sign. She walked calmly to the elevators while Rudy and I slipped out via the back stairs.

I did get some rest when Nancy took me home but not much since Nancy joined me in bed. (My headache had no effect on my other bodily functions.) Up to this point I've been reluctant to reveal our bedroom intimacies, but now I have no choice but to stray from that policy a little. For, one time during our pleasure that afternoon I saw her say my name. (Her hands were too busy elsewhere to be signing.) (Even in poor lighting and distracting circumstances I can lip read my name.)

If locker room conversation can be believed, Nancy's action was not at all unusual. Either because of that or because I was too occcupied, the implications didn't sink in right away. But later, when Nancy was asleep and I was resting, one of those "aha" insights hit me. However, it didn't come as an "aha" but more as a combination of "oh, no" and "holy shit." What happened was that I connected two other remarks that had been made to me at different times, by different people, in different contexts.

"It's a good thing she couldn't hear what I said." (Tom—see page 38.)

"You're not the only person who can lip read." (Charlotte—see page 69.)

Do you understand my "oh, no" now? Aton was guilty as hell and I had no plans to abandon my chase but maybe, just maybe, he wasn't guilty of Sarah's murder. If not, the murderer was one of my "team." Depending on what might happen my life could depend on our teamwork. What if one of the players was more than just unreliable?

14

The sun had been set for half an hour when I pulled into Viktor's parking lot. There were several other empty spaces and no Private-Property-You-Will-Be-Towed signs, so I felt reasonably sure that my car would still be there when I got back. If anything, it was my return that was questionable. People who shoot at other people miss more often in the movies than in real life. If Aton were around and took another shot, I didn't fancy my chances. Rudy had saved my life the first time but I was about to head into enemy territory all alone. My head still hurt and the doctor said I should be in the hospital. Instead, I was going on a commando raid. As I've said before, there are less-than-rational parts of my mind.

The Visitors Welcome sign was still in place but there was a chain across the drive. It seemed that the University of the Sun only welcomed visitors when the sun was up. All the more reason for my nocturnal visit. I hopped the chain and walked beside the trees off the road, but on as solid ground as I could find. It's hard for me to know how much noise I'm making when I walk through the woods. My rough guide is that the larger the twig I feel myself breaking, the louder the noise. Hearing friends have told me that stepping on leaves makes noise too, though softer. Brittle leaves are supposed to crackle louder but it's hard to feel the difference between leaves through one's shoes.

I walked, therefore, slowly and carefully. I was in no particular hurry. I continually looked up, down, and around me. I'd worn the darkest clothing I'd brought to California, dark blue jeans and sweatshirt, and hoped that would help. With one exception, I had no specific plan, no single piece of information I was looking for. I just felt that there was something wrong under the University of the Sun and I wanted to find out what.

The visitors center was, as I expected, closed. It was also locked. I should have expected that too and come prepared somehow. Since I hadn't, and I'm neither a burglar or locksmith by trade or avocation, the locked door presented a problem. The only window was high out of reach and the adobe walls were sheer.

What I wanted to see was the contents of the filing cabinet, but even if I found a way in I'd probably find the cabinet locked too. I couldn't see any alarm but that didn't mean that there wasn't any. I couldn't see any solution so I put the visitors center on hold and walked around the hill toward the pyramids.

I could see a light from the entrance of the completed pyramid but the unfinished one was dark. It seemed less likely that I'd learn something in the half-done pyramid but also less likely that I'd be caught. I didn't relish the idea of capture (and ensuing torture or death?) so that was where I started. It was easy to cross the open space in the dim moonlight and step inside unobserved.

I'd brought a small flashlight, fortunately, because without it I wouldn't have been able to see. The walls of the pyramid shut out the moon and the electricity had not yet been installed so the inside was proverbially pitch black. The only things I could see were what was hit by the beam of my light.

I don't consider myself paranoic but being alone in the dark pyramid was making it hard to investigate. The farther I strayed from the entrance the more I worried. Perhaps I'd have been better off if I hadn't known that the Egyptian pyramids were built as massive tombs for the pharoahs. They held the mummified bodies of the man-gods, gold and other precious jewels, and safeguards against grave robbers. Had Aton, Tut, and Sphinx installed any traps, pitfalls, or safeguards in their pyramids? If so, to protect what?

Because I was afraid, I pushed myself to go on. I had a job to do and could not let unreasonable fear keep me back.

(Another aside about English—there's a word for the fear of the number 13, 'triskaidekaphobia', but no word for the more common fear of the dark. Strange.) One "advantage" I had was that if some door were to clang shut and locked behind me, (an almost obligatory scene in scary movies), I wouldn't hear it. Overcoming a fear is a challenge. I like to test myself, both physically and mentally and moving forward in the dark crypt was part both. I had to tell my legs to move, then actually move them.

And this challenge was important because it was about something important. I was trying to save a friend's life and better my character at the same time. Playing my best and smartest in racquetball was a trivial challenge in comparison.

To my best estimate, the floor plan of the second pyramid was a duplicate of the completed one. It was hard, however, to put together a big picture based on the information I was gleaning from the single-beam illumination. Also, I had not been shown all of the first pyramid. I found what seemed to be the library, the cafeteria, and a corridor of student rooms.

Then I got lost.

I remembered each turn I had made but I hadn't been counting footsteps. Nor had I been dropping pebbles as I walked or in any other way marked the path I had taken. On heading back from what seemed to be another corridor of student rooms I must have made a turn too soon or too late. Once I wasn't back at the library when I was supposed to be, I was in trouble.

I'm not phobic about the night but that doesn't mean I like it. My awareness starts with my eyes and when their effectiveness is reduced I'm less comfortable. And I don't like getting lost. Getting lost means I've made a mistake. I make mistakes often but never like to. I tell my students to take their mistakes in stride and learn from them but I'm harder on myself. This California adventure was becoming a more and more humbling experience.

After swearing at myself I figured I'd try to make the best of it and see what I'd stumbled into. Whenever there was an opening that looked like a room, I went in and probed with the beam. In each case I got the same result—nothing. The rooms were empty. I had entered the unfinished pyramid and that was exactly what I found—an unfinished pyramid. The secrets of the University of the Sun weren't there. (Because the "students" were in and around all of it during the building process?) My answers would be in the fully operative pyramid with Tut, Sphinx, and Aton.

I don't know how I found my way out but I know that I was sweating (and not from the weather) when I did. I just kept walking and sweeping my beam ahead of me. The building was only so big and if worst came to worst the builders and the sun would return and I would try to escape then. After an hour of wandering (not 40 years) I found myself back at the entrance. I was relieved to be unlost but upset at myself for wasting so much time. It had been two and a half hours since I'd parked at Viktor's.

There was only one structure left to search so I walked to it. The faint light was still showing from the entrance. Like the unfinished pyramid, and unlike the visitors center, there was no locked door guarding the entrance, in fact, no door at all. I stepped in softly. No one rushed up to attack me. Apparently I'd entered unheard. (I owe what ability I have to move silently to a leadership training program sponsored by the Junior National Association of the Deaf. I had to be taught that sliding chairs, closing doors, etc. make noise while sunshine is silent.)

Cautiously, I walked to the library to orient myself and plan. It had a door, without a lock, but the door was open anyway. The overhead light was on dimly, it was what I had seen when I'd walked around the hill. It was the middle of the night and the rest of the pyramid was dark though occupied by Tut, Sphinx, and an unknown number of students and faculty. And Aton? With his gun?

As I was thinking, out of the corner of my eye I saw Sphinx in the hallway. In an opthamologist's office my (and other deaf people's) vision wouldn't test out as unusual but I guarantee you that I use my sight to the maximum. I've known hearing people who notice as much in front of them as I do, but no one who sees as much peripherally. (Tom tends to bump into things as we walk down the street signing.) I don't claim

94

that better trained eyes compensate for unfunctioning ears, (Rudy's hearing had saved my life.), but at the University of the Sun my own senses and quick reaction saved me from who knows what.

I had been leaning against one wall, not a straight on view from the doorway. I slipped behind the door just in time. I put my eye low to the crack between the door and the wall. Sphinx poked her head in the room, gave a perfunctory look around, then left. I walked around to the doorway and poked my own head out (Behold the turtle. It makes progress only when it sticks its neck out.) to look in the direction Sphinx had gone. She was doing the same thing to the other rooms— glancing in to see if everything was all right.

It wasn't much, but I'd just learned my first piece of information for the night. One little part of the riddle of Sphinx was solved. At least one of her roles was that of a sentry. Her size and musculature were probably not coincidences.

Sphinx's patrol duty strengthened my conviction that there was something untoward to be learned at the U. of S. but made me realize that I couldn't learn it in the middle of the night, or at least that night. The visitor's center had been locked. The unfinished pyramid hadn't yielded any secrets and was unlikely to do so. The pyramid in use was patrolled. I had been lucky in seeing Sphinx before she had seen me. If I prowled around more my luck would probably run out. (Only James Bond seems to have an unlimited supply of luck.)

So, three strikes and I was out. I didn't like the result but I was stuck with it. It was a failure I had to accept. As quietly as I could, I left the pyramid and the entire university. My car was still there, waiting for me, at Viktor's.

I was not, however, despondent. To continue my baseball analogy, I had only struck out once. I planned to come back to the University of the Sun for another turn at bat.

I needed and wanted to learn more. There are many ways to learn. The best method depends on the circumstances. My master's degree notwithstanding, I felt that in a day or two the time was ripe for me to go back to college.

15

When I got home the sun was just making its appearance over the Berkeley hills. I let myself in with the spare key Nancy had given me. I was as silent as I know how to be. I flopped myself down on the couch in the war room and fell asleep quickly.

Nancy tapped me on the shoulder to rouse me. "Why are you sleeping here?"

"I didn't want to wake you. What time is it?"

"I wouldn't have minded. It's eight now. I have to go work at Cody's this morning. I've called in sick too often recently. They'll get suspicious if I do it again today."

Do you have time to fill me in on what you and Rudy found out yesterday then make a fast sick call to my boss for me?"

"Sure. We found out just what you suspected. About half the people we reached had been contacted by the University of the Sun, either by phone, in person, or by mail. But no one made any complaints about pressure or harrassment."

"I didn't think there would be any. Californians are susceptible to the soft sell. People on the heliotherapy center mailing list are prime candidates for the University of the Sun."

"What did you find out?"

"Almost nothing, only that there is something to find out. I'm going back tomorrow, to enroll. Today I have some other errands I have to take care of."

"Like what?"

"Seeing Tom, and his lawyer. Those I'll do myself. Can we make that call to Washington now? I'll pay you for it later."

"Sure, but don't worry about the money."

It took a while to get properly connected. My boss wasn't in his office and since he couldn't be paged they had to send someone to search for him, then find a secretary to interpret. Eventually, however, we were ready to communicate. (Methodolgically, that is. I had a funny feeling that the call would take a turn I wouldn't like.)

"Hi boss. Sorry to force this double interpreter situation on us but I don't have access to a T.D.D."

"That's okay. Where are you now?"

"California, and I'm sick."

"How convenient to be sick in California."

"No, honest, I am. As you know, I came out here to solve a murder. I haven't done that yet but I did manage to get shot at. I was brought to the hospital Saturday night, unconscious. I'm out of danger now but I have a concussion and the doctor ordered me to stay for a few days of observation."

"That sounds like something too wild for you to make up as an excuse."

"I knew you'd understand."

"So, I'll put you down as on sick leave."

"Fine. I'll be back as soon as I can."

"And I expect you to come back with a note from the doctor."

"Shit," I said. "Nancy don't interpret that." (Luckily, Nancy wasn't a professional interpreter. She obeyed me. If she knew and followed the interpreter's code of ethics she'd have had to convey to my boss exactly what I said. "Shit, Nancy don't interpret that.")

"Okay," I said, asking Nancy to start interpreting again, "Will do. See you soon."

"I hope so."

Nancy left for Cody's and I went to Jefferson's office, with a pit stop at Eclair. The nourishment helped alleviate the lack of sleep. It was early in the morning, so I caught him in.

"Good morning Mr. Jefferson. Do you have a few minutes?"

"Yes, but I have no new information to give you."

"What about the alibis of the four people whose names I gave you?"

"I have been able to get responses from only three. I haven't been able to reach this 'Aton' fellow."

"That's okay. I figured that. I have some information to give you about him, but what about the other three?"

"None have an alibi that can be verified. In fact, all three claim they were doing the same thing. They all say that they were at home reading."

On any given Friday night in California, and all over America, there will be millions of people sitting at home reading, often including me. But all three of my suspect-friends on the very night of the murder? Two out of three would be more likely. Also, that all three said the same thing reminded me of a captioned movie that I had seen. It was an adaptation of an Agatha Christie book, *Murder on the Orient Express*, where they all did it. That didn't seem possible in this case, but that's still what came to mind.

I filled Jefferson in on all my investigating and about the attempt on my life. He didn't like my plan to go back to school.

"You told Sergeant Grimsley you'd let the police do the police work."

"I am, I'm just satisfying my need for more knowledge at the most interesting and unusual 'university' that I've ever come across."

"Why don't you tell the sergeant about your suspicions and let her investigate."

"She'll find nothing wrong."

"And you think you will?"

"I hope so. I'll be watched, I'm sure, but I'll have more time and more flexibility."

"Have you considered that another attempt might be made on your life?"

"Yes, but after the first miss I doubt there'll be anything blatant. If he persists, he'll probably try to make me have an 'accident'. I'll be careful. And I'll keep you posted whenever I learn anything."

"I'm still not happy with the idea, but I doubt I could stop you."

"Right."

"In that case, please do keep in touch."

"I will."

"In the mean time, I'll keep in contact with Sergeant Grimsley to see what the police have learned."

"Fine. Thank you for all your help."

"It's my job."

"Thanks anyway."

I brought my *Hitchhiker's Guide* . . . to the jail. It had made me laugh and if there's any place that can use laughter, it's a jail. Tom thanked me for it and said he'd read it later. What was most important to him, of course, was the progress of the investigation.

I told him about everything: Aton's other name, the shooting, and the University of the Sun. He listened passively until I said that I also suspected Charlotte.

"She couldn't have done it."

"Why not?"

"I know her."

"What do you know about her? Where she works—yes. The basic biography of her life—yes. How she acts when she's with you—yes. How much knowledge is that really? She was jealous of Sarah, wasn't she?"

"Yes, but. . . "

"Well."

"Jealousy and murder are different," he said.

"I know that and I don't know if she did it or not. I'm just trying to examine and test all possibilities and I want you to do the same."

"What about *your* new woman, Nancy. You said she was jealous of Sarah too."

100

Nancy. I hadn't suspected her seriously since we'd bedded. I'd noticed that every time we were alone and I'd brought up the case she rushed me into bed, but I'd discounted that. I prefer sex to talking about murder too. I didn't see how she could have done it but I couldn't say any more in her defense than Tom had said for Charlotte.

"Touché," I said. "I haven't ruled her out either."

"What about Alexis?"

He saved my life, remember. But yes, everyone, including him, is still a suspect until I know for sure."

"Except me?"

"Right, except you."

"Why?"

"Because I know you."

"Hmmm," he said. that sounds familiar. Wasn't I saying that about Charlotte and weren't you criticizing me for it?"

"Oh, shut up. I have to get back to work—not my job, but your case."

"Then get moving. Get out of here," his jocular tone then stopped, "but come back soon. When you see Charlotte, tell her to visit."

"I will, and I will."

I had time for a long lunch before Charlotte was due in Berkeley. It had been a full week since I'd been to Los Burritos so that's where I headed. Most of the time I eat alone I have a book or crossword puzzle with me. (In the East when I read and eat at a restaurant I'm looked at as odd. In San Francisco Bay I'm just part of the crowd.) At Los Burritos, however, I perused no printed matter. While the burritos were food for my belly a very serious puzzle was food for my thought. Or perhaps two puzzles. The two questions would have two answers but there might be a cause-and-effect or some other relationship between them. What kind of fraud, mind-control, or other no-good was happening at the University of the Sun? and Who killed Sarah?

Why? could be asked about both issues but for the first it was hardly necessary. The answer seemed clear and it was not indigineous or limited to California—money. But was greed (and the need to cover one's tracks) the why to Sarah's murder too? If so, then there was only one puzzle. If I had been right with my first guess, jealousy, then there were two.

There were some smaller questions, small pieces of the jigsaw that if I answered might give me some direction.

(1) How much did Charlotte know or suspect about Tom's love for Sarah?

(2) What was Sarah's relationship to Nancy? They didn't seem to be friends but Sarah had been teaching her sign language.

(3) What were (or rather, had been) Sarah's feelings for Rudy?

(4) What kind of control did Aton have over Sarah—and over others at the University of the Sun?

(5) Why didn't Sphinx speak?

(6) What was Tut's role?

There was a road to take to find those answers—Rte. 1. They would be at the University of the Sun. I'd be going there the next day.

There was another question tugging at my mind too. It was not related to the case, or only tangentially, but it bothered me. How would Nancy react when I went back to Washington? I liked her and she was the best bed-mate I'd ever had. Yet I'd leave her and return east. No matter how nice, I couldn't see a permanent relationship with a woman who believed in heliotherapy. I'd never said that to her and doubted that I could. When she asked me to stay, as I was sure she would, I'd have to find some less painful lie. Shit. Relationships are always complicated. Maybe I don't know how to manage my affairs with women any better than Tom.

When I'm not sexually and/or romantically involved I'm a lot more sure of myself. Even with women like Charlotte. I met her at Nancy's at about 3:30. I told her what Rudy, Nancy, and I found out about the University of the Sun, and my plan to return as a student. I said I'd keep her informed and that Tom wanted her to visit. I had nothing more to say to her, nor her to me, so our conversation was short and sweet.

That evening Nancy and I did something together that was not sex, food, or crime detection. We saw a movie. The movie, however, involved all of the above and was so incredible (in the original meaning of "incapable of being believed") as to be silly and insulting. I won't waste space describing Mr. Bond's death defying feats. And even though I'm a man I found the title, "Octopussy" to be offensive.

In spite of the quality of the movie, it was a nice evening. I needed the break and it showed Nancy that I was interested in more than just her body and her ability to help me communicate. (I didn't let her interpret the movie for me. She was my date, not my interpreter.) It was the kind of change and activity that helped me feel and think better. My headaches even seemed to diminish in intensity.

After the show we returned to sleep and play on the waterbed. In the morning I felt awake, alert, and refreshed but also a little nervous. I was to become a student again. I was on the way to my very first day at my new school.

16

Tut and Sphinx were taken aback at my entrance. As when Rudy and I had visited, there were no other tourists at the visitors center.

"Hello," said Tut. "How nice to see you again. How can we help you?"

"I'd like to enroll."

I have to give them credit for a good try at concealing their reactions. The expressions of disbelief lasted only a fraction of a second before they were replaced with smiles, but I saw their amazement and I think they knew it.

"What good news. Let me get an application."

The application came in two parts. The first asked for your basic data: name, address, phone number, employer, etc. The second was called a C.F.S. form, C.F.S. for Confidential Financial Statement. It's a long one, but all the questions boil down to one—How much are you worth? Worth includes cash, salary, house, stocks, insurance policies, income from parental support, everything.

It took me half an hour to fill out mine and I did it honestly. I handed it to them and watched to see their reactions. I suspected the confidential tuition policy to be something like a tithe. After filling out my form I hoped that to be the case. If so, they'd have interesting facial expressions because the University of the Sun would have to give me a scholarship. I have a six month old car, but the bank owns it. I have a nice apartment, but I rent. My furniture was purchased either at Goodwill Industries or the Salvation Army. I own no jewelry, coins, or stamps. My most valuable possesions are my paperback books. (I have a signed original hardcover edition of *Dune* worth about $300 but I forgot to mention that on the application.)

And I have bills—Visa, MasterCard, American Express, Student Loans, etc. I checked my math, put down my net worth on the bottom line, then circled it.—$271. In my opinion that's not a bad figure since I have a steady job, but Tut didn't seem pleased when she scanned the papers.

"These seem to be complete."

"They are."

"Well, only Chancellor Aton can make final decisions concerning admissions and he's not here now. When would you like to start?"

"Now."

"Today?"

"Yes. Right now. I feel lost. I'm being pressured to return East which I feel would destroy the small core of inner peace that I have. I'm afraid that if I leave the grounds this afternoon I'll fall under the pernicious influence of my friends and family on the backward East Coast. They don't understand the spirit of California."

"I see. Well, I am authorized to grant you a temporary and conditional acceptance, subject to the approval of the chancellor, with the tuition to be determined by him, and assign you a mentor. Would that be acceptable?"

I missed some of her words but caught enough to know she was telling me—Yes, for now. "That would be fine," I said.

"Welcome to the University of the Sun," Tut said. She rose and shook my hand. Your mentor will be Sphinx. Follow her."

Sphinx smiled.

She led me to a vacant room. Her gestures told me it was to be mine. It was bare except for the sleeping pallet, desk, and lamp. I had brought a few essentials in a back pack. (I like packs since they leave my hands free to sign.) At Sphinx's suggestion I left the room and followed her. She brought me to the library and bade me to sit down. I complied and she brought me a stack of books.

Apparently, as a initiation, I was to start with a "familiar" eternal mystery—Stonehenge. I hadn't read any of the books but I knew one of the authors, John Fowles, and had enjoyed his *The French Lieutenant's Woman*. I started to plow into all the possible theories and explanations for the standing stones but frequently let my eyes drift over the pages.

What I wanted to do was get to know and converse with other students. What were their reasons for enrolling? I assumed mine were unique. What did they get from the University of the Sun? There were about a dozen young men and women in the library with me. (I'd seen many others constructing the new Pyramid as Sphinx and I walked from the visitors center.) What I wanted to do was to walk up to one, introduce myself, and start to chat. When I tried that, however, I found that my "mentor" did not permit it.

Sphinx never left my side. When I sat at the table and read, so did she. When I tried to approach another student she interposed her body between us and pointed to a sign on the wall, which stated rule number one of the University of the Sun—Thou Shalt Not Interrupt the Learning or Meditation of Another. She did permit me to go to the bathroom alone but she followed me to the door and waited there for me until I was through.

I tried to pick up information, therefore, by reading the facial expressions and body language of the other students. We deaf people are good at that. I noticed one peculiarity at the University of the Sun and I continued to see it for the duration of my matriculation.

At Gallaudet and any other university I've seen there is a commonality visible in the majority of the students. Their bodies and faces show gaiety, lightheartedness, spirit, pep, or whatever you want to call it. Even in the depths of the library, where serious study is noticed, there's an intensity in the faces of the readers.

The University of the Sun was different. Tut had talked (others still do) of the pyramid's power to add vitality and energy to one's life forces, but that's not what I saw. The students at the University of the Sun looked listless. These were not the crazy, freaky, floaty, bouncy Californians (whether native, transplanted, or spiritual) that I knew. Something was wrong but I didn't know what.

The dining room was a bit cheerier. Maybe there is something to the natural food movement. There was talk and more animation in the faces of my compatriots. Students sat in randomly assorted groups, except me. I was still alone with Sphinx. It seemed that her presence was either a signal or warning to the others not to join us. The food was unrecognizable to me, either in looks or in taste. It was bland but edible. Sphinx also tried to make sure that I took my vitamins but I remembered that they were made from seaweed so the two pills stayed in the roof of my mouth till I went to the bathroom. I was about to throw and flush them down the toilet but on a whim stashed them in my pocket instead.

After dinner, till lights out, was more study. It's hard to explain Stonehenge by coincidence. The odds would be astronomical. To me, however, all the other explanations seemed no more likely, no better than chance. If Sphinx asked me to write a paper I would illuminate a theory I felt as plausible as any ohter. Namely, the placement of the stones was caused by an errant throw of an extra-terrestrial bowler who then had to leave the alleys in a hurry when its spouse located it and summoned it home to help with the dinner dishes.

There didn't seem to be an official bed time but around 10:00 all the students began to drift out. I stayed but when all the others had gone Sphinx made it clear that she wanted us to go to my room. I obeyed.

Perhaps it was Tut's turn for sentry duty because Sphinx didn't leave me at my door. I was hoping that as a student I could do some more successful night exploration than I had as an invader, but my mentor's presence changed all that. When I first realized that Sphinx didn't plan to leave there was an awkward time, as there so often is. I was sure she was as aware as I was that there was only one sleeping pallet.

Sex with Nancy, as with most women, produces in me a whole spectrum of emotions: horniness, doubt, pride, guilt. It's never the same. How much do I feel? How does she feel? Is there an us? Why am I complicating my life this way? I want this night to last forever. etc.

With Sphinx, everything was different. The awkward moment lasted only a short time. As soon as she sensed it, she undressed, slowly, then lay on the (my?) sleeping pallet and waited for me.

There was no spectrum of emotions in me then, just two. One was normal and familiar—lust. Her silence, her beauty, and her body (all six foot four inches of it) were tantalizing and irresistible. Despite what was running through my mind, my lust and her invitation left no doubt about what I would do. I undressed and joined her.

What was fucking my mind, however, was something I'd never experienced before with a woman—suspicion. Why was Sphinx doing this, a part of the plot to keep "students" here and bleed their money? Was this a deliberate method to keep me from roaming? Was I under closer surveillance than a normal student? Would a femal student be provided with a male mentor? Suppose a student, male or female, didn't want sexual mentorship? Was there a knife under the pallet that Sphinx knew about and was planning to use?

Whatever, I didn't hesitate or hold back. There are probably better and stronger men, men who would have told Sphinx to go to hell and kicked her out of bed, (if that were possible at her size and strength), but not me. This was not love. There was no iota or even pretense of it from either of us. For me the situation became a simple one. For the mindfuck she was putting on me, I wanted to get what I was paying for.

The scene at breakfast was the same as the one at dinner—including my chicanery with my vitamins. Faces were alert, the conversation reasonably animated, the food bland. Sphinx, and only Sphinx, was my mealtime companion.

I didn't look forward to another day of valueless study and reading, nor the prospect of facing Aton—if he was due to show up. What could I learn this way? I'd flopped on my secret night mission (impossible?) and didn't want to fail again.

I was led back to the library and the Stonehenge books after breakfast. I kept the books open and my eyes on the page, but my mind on the problem of how to proceed, what to do. Sphinx calmly read one of her own mysterious books.

Knowledge is a funny thing. Knowing all the facts is often not enough. You have to know what you know. The jigsaw puzzle analogy, where you have all the pieces and need to put them together properly, has been used often but there's more to it than that. Some facts are irrelevant, some important, some vital. All pieces are not equal. You can get the big picture without some details.

I didn't get any illumination, insight, brainstorm inspiration, or afflatus about any *eternal* mystery that morning, but the University of the Sun somehow became clear to me. The answer, the key pieces, had been in the faces of the students, and, in my pocket. I had wasted a lot of time meditating on the "mystery" of Sphinx's silence—silly me.

Sudden awareness is always a mixed emotion. There's the pleasing "Now I understand," but also the accompanying "Dummy, why didn't you think of that before." Both feelings were strong in me then.

I tried to hide the delight part from my face since I had another problem left—how to escape. Tut had said that students were free to leave at any time. Bullshit. It would be true on one level for the others but I didn't think for a moment that they'd let me go. Even though they didn't know that I knew what they were up to, I'd been too nosy, too prying, too cynical.

I could think of only the most primitive way out but sometimes the most basic and obvious strategy is what's necessary. "I need some sun," I told Sphinx.

She followed me as I walked outside. I told her I needed some exercise, and did some bends to touch my toes, then some jumping jacks. Sphinx just watched. I limbered up till I felt good and loose. Then I ran.

I expected Sphinx to chase me, and she did. I had the head start my surprise tactic had afforded me. I'm fast for an amateur athlete, but no Olympic sprinter. Sphinx probably has the potential for the women's games since she overtook me before I reached my car, parked across from the visitors center. She was a better athlete than me but I have quite a varied background. I'd played one sport that, apparently, she hadn't. Football. I know how to break tackles. She came at me too high so I used her own momentum and a stiff arm to send her sprawling.

It didn't give me a lot of time, she recovered quickly, but just enough to get locked in my car and the engine going. They hadn't been wise enough to take away my keys and other personal items. Thank you, University of the Sun, for that mistake. Sphinx couldn't tackle my car either so I sped down palm row with no one following me.

I must have seen Aton's car heading toward me a split second before he saw mine heading toward him. Otherwise I doubt I'd have been able to avoid the blocking maneuver he tried. As it was, I still had to sideswipe my car against a tree to pass him. (I didn't care about that since the car belonged to Avis and I'd paid three bucks extra for collision insurance.)

I assumed, correctly as it turned out, that he would turn around and follow me. When I was on the main road going south, driving far faster than I liked, I could see him in the distance, through my rear view mirror.

When you're driving faster than you're comfortable doing you pay closest attention to staying on the road and seeing what is directly in front of you. You can miss things to the side, like I did. I missed the turn off for the longer, safer road that I'd used before on my return from the University of the Sun. Instead, I found myself back in the mountains, on Rte. 1, southbound, in the cliffside lane. Aton was not far behind me, and was gaining. He had the faster, better handling car. He had the Celica, I still had my rented Escort.

Great, I thought. You've escaped the clutches of the university only to put yourself in a worse position. I didn't know if Aton had a gun, but he didn't need one. A shove off the road would provide a convenient accident. Murder might be suspected but impossible to prove. If Avis equipped their cars with wings I'd have a perfect escape route. Since they didn't, I didn't fancy my chances.

There was one condition, however, that was helping me. It was a nice sunshiny morning and there were other cars on the road. There were only two between us southbound but the fairly steady stream going northbound to the beaches and Point Reyes made it nearly impossible to pass. Passing was illegal but I doubted he cared much for that prohibition. As soon as he could squeeze and swerve through to me, he would.

The other cars also helped me by slowing both me and Aton down. I could take some mental energy off just staying on the road and put it into planning. What would he try? Ramming or sideswiping? What could I do against either?

He found a momentary break in the northbound traffic and passed one of the cars between us. I still couldn't think of a plan. Five minutes later there was another break and he passed the last obstacle. He was right on my tail.

I don't often think about death. I go through my days enjoying what I have. When someone asks me, "Don't you worry about heaven or hell or what will happen to you when you die?" I have a ready response. "No," I say, "I'll be dead then." When Aton rammed my rear fender, however, I did think about death, thought about it intensely.

"Thought," though, isn't the right word. What was happening in my head wasn't connected to words, signs, or language at all. Very simply, I didn't want to die. I didn't pray but I was scared, for it looked as if I would die. I couldn't see a way out. At his next opportunity, I'd be sideswiped and nudged off the cliff.

Maybe my lack of planning helped me. Maybe my atheism helped. If I'd been asking someone/thing to help me I might have put just a little less than my all into helping myself. I don't know. Maybe it was just sheer luck.

Whatever, I took advantage of a long shot, a situation provided by a peculiar twist of the road and an oncoming mobile home in the other lane. As Aton jockeyed to get into a spot at my side I did something unexpected. I sped up, swerved, and drove across the road into the mountain. Just before I crashed I saw Aton had stayed in the "passing" lane just a little too long. The camper hit him and sent him skidding out of control. The car that had previously been between he and I in our lane couldn't stop in time and barreled into his car while it was skidding. He had no chance. I saw him slide over the edge and then the mountain rushed up to meet me.

17

The crash solved one of my problems. I didn't need to worry about a doctor's note. My second stay in California hospital was not a mere overnight visit, it was a week. My memories of that week, especially the first few days, are vague.

I thought I'd had headaches before. Was I ever wrong. Only in sleep, blissful sleep, would the man or woman operating a jackhammer inside my head stop. I remember having visitors: Nancy, Rudy, Charlotte, and Sergeant Grimsley shortly after I arrived. I remember being lucid enough at some point to tell the sergeant to check my vitamins. I drifted in and out of sleep, semi-sleep, and brief spells of awareness. The closer to awake I was, the greater the pain.

Besides the aggravated concussion I'd bruised two ribs and broken a leg. I learned later that I'd been on the critical list for a day and a half, but I didn't know it at the time. As soon as I could see that I was in a hospital, I felt I'd live. Only Aton had died.

After a few days, when I was recovered enough to read, I was brought a newspaper. It had an upsetting and unsettling story about me (partly) entitled "Multi-Car Crash on Rte. 1 Kills One, Injurs Three.' Among the injured, the paper said, was one Robert Brewer of Washington, D.C. I didn't recognize the names of the other injured, but I did recognize the dead man's name. John Smith, of San Francisco.

It was trivial, but it irked me. It was just one more thing I'd been wrong about. Though it wasn't important, I'd been sure that "Smith" was just another alias. From the short obituary it was clear that John Smith had been Aton's given name. Assumptions again, I'd have to do a better job at them.

But that inconsequential mistake was only a minor irritation. What bothered me was that I'd injured two other people, innocent bystanders. One had been released after treatment for abrasions and lacerations, but the other was in critical condition with a fractured skull. The cause of the accident was listed as "unclear" but that Mr. Brewer's car had seemed to go out of control (untrue), crossing the highway. Which, of course, led to everything else.

I didn't feel guilty at all about Aton's death. It was self defense and was his second attempt on my life. But the means of escape that *I* chose had fractured another man's skull. (My skull was only jarred. People have always told me I'm hard-headed.) What responsibility did I have to that man who'd been minding his own business? What if he died?

In a way, I'm glad it was a while before I could think clearly. Contemplating the death of an innocent, by my hands, however forced, was not something I wanted to do. This was not a trip to California that I'd want to remember, but I would. And it was not over.

Eventually, I was awake and alert most of the time, with only slightly diminshed pain. I could even walk, though wobbily, with the walking cast that had been put on me. The headaches continued. They were omni-present and severe but didn't interfere with my functioning. I could do what I had to do as long as I could ignore the pain. I was "lucky" enough that the leg I'd broken was my left one. I could even drive, once I got out of the hospital.

At the end of that very long week Nancy and Sergeant Grimsley came together for a visit. Nancy spoke first about some practical things. She had had the hospital call my boss and send a letter to my job. She sent Charlotte to the jail to let Tom know where I was. She called Avis. She called Tom's lawyer to let him know what had happened. And—she had gotten permission from the doctors to take me home as soon as Sergeant Grimsley was finished.

116

"Thanks," I said. "I'm going stir crazy here. And thanks for the errands too. Sergeant, fire away. The sooner I'm out of the hospital and home with this wonderful woman, (Nancy smiled) the happier I'll be."

"I really don't have questions." Sergeant Grimsley spoke and Nancy interpreted for me. "I have some information, though. There is no more University of the Sun. I had the spirulina tablets analysed at the lab and they found the addictive poison that you must have suspected. It's a depressant, after the initial stimulation fades. Subjects feel euphoric and content for a while then become docile and malleable."

"That explains everything," I said, "the inertia, the cheerfulness at meals, how they rob people blind, how they get them to sweat and strain to build stupid pyramids, and why me and my suspicions had to be eliminated."

"Right. Mr. Smith's two associates, Susan O'Neill and Dorothy Weingarten, are in jail."

"Who was Tut and who was Sphinx?"

"What?"

"Nothing important, just a part of the whole game. John Smith used the Egyptian alias Aton and the women used Tut and Sphinx. Sphinx even acted mute to 'mimic' the great Egyptian stone sphinx. They were so blatant it was silly. Only gullible, drugged, dopes could be duped by such a farce. To switch topics, what about the other man injured in the accident? Will he live?"

"His condition is critical, but stable."

"Will there be any charges brought against me?"

"For what?"

"Reckless driving? Manslaughter? Something?"

"No. Circumstances were beyond your control."

"I don't know about that, but thank you. Has Tom Hayes been released?"

"No."

"No?"

"I did keep your suspicions in mind. Mr. Smith was at the University of the Sun on the night Sarah Collins was murdered. Not only Ms. O'Neill and Ms. Weingarten claim that, several 'students' too. The clincher was corroboration by the proprietor of a local restaurant."

"Viktor?"

"Yes."

"Shit."

Sergeant Grimsley was silent. I didn't apologize, but I did explain myself. "That means that Smith was there. The others could be a conspiracy but I've met Viktor. If he said he saw John Smith, then he saw him."

That's what we believe. I'm sorry about your friend Mr. Hayes, but the Marin county police are especially pleased with the evidence you gave them to shut down the University of the Sun."

"Tom's still innocent."

"I wish I could believe that, but I don't."

"Then I still have work to do."

"But not police work."

"Of course not."

I went back with Nancy and I was silent for the whole ride home. I wasn't well physically and was feeling worse about myself. Because of some good fortune I'd exposed a silly fraud and helped some people who'd be likely to join some other cult in a few weeks. In the process, Rudy acquired a bullet in the shoulder and a stranger a fractured skull. I'd succumbed to a disgusting night of lust with "Sphinx" while a good woman, who I was planning to leave, was treating me right. And I hadn't freed Tom. If I were generous, I could perhaps grade my performance and behavior in California as an F+.

Worst of all was the distressing problem left for me that Sarah's murderer was one of three people, none of whom I wanted it to be. Rudy was a new friend who had saved my life, Nancy a woman who seemed to love me, and Charlotte a fellow deafie. (No, I never for a minute considered that Tom could be guilty as charged.) How in hell can anyone work as a detective for a living? It's beyond me.

Once we got home, Nancy asked me what was wrong, why I was so quiet, and I didn't know what to say.

"Tom's still in jail," I tried. "Look at all the time I've wasted and the grief I've caused others."

"Grief?! You saved all those innocent people at the University of the Sun and restored the image and credibility of the Heliotherapy Center."

"Great."

"No. Really. You're wonderful." She was able to drag me to bed and, in a technical way, get me to make love to her but my heart wasn't in it. I was tired in body and in soul. I wanted to do nothing more than take the next plane east. I was sick of California. I wanted my safe, sane, life and job in the nation's capital. I was tired of adults and murder. As aggravating as teenagers can be, they're fun to work with. I had a job and a social life in Washington and though there was an overlap, as there inevitably is with deaf people who work in service to the deaf, it wasn't as hoplessly entangled as this California web.

I stayed, however, because of Tom and my pride. He was my friend. I'd told him I'd get him out of jail and, damn it, I would. I stayed in bed with Nancy overnight and by myself all the next morning. I took my time getting ready. Nancy had taken the bus to Cody's and left me the car. I borrowed it to drive down to Fremont to confront Charlotte.

On the way I thought but not in the abstract about assumptions or knowledge or degrees of truth. I needed to think about specifics. Which of my three suspects was not at home reading that night? What did Sarah do from the time she and Tom argued at lunch till the time she was killed? Who followed her to Tom's and how did he or she get in? And, how could I find out?

I arrived a few minutes before school let out so I'd be certain to catch her. I waited for all her students to leave, then wambled in.

"You again," she said. "I thought you were in the hospital."

"I was, until yesterday afternoon. My head aches, my ribs hurt, and I don't like walking with a cast on my leg."

"Poor boy. So why did you come?"

"First, because I'm sick and tired of California. Second, to talk about books. What was the name of the book you were reading on the night Sarah was murdered?"

"How am I supposed to remember? And how do you know it was a book? Couldn't it have been a magazine or a newspaper?"

"Excuse me, I stand corrected. Do you happen to remember what printed matter you were reading that night?"

"Nothing important, just some murder mystery."

"Cute, very cute. I can now see one thing Tom saw in you. With your wit, I'm sure he was never bored."

"Thank you for the lovely compliment."

"Enough bullshit. It pains me to think that a deaf person could be a murderer but for you, I might be willing to make an exception."

"Don't fret. You have no cause to worry. Great sleuth that you are, you've surmised correctly that I wasn't home reading. In fact, I drove up to Berkeley—McGee Ave. to be specific, but I didn't kill her. She was dead when I got there.

"You'll be pleased to know that I didn't go to Berkeley to see her, much less kill her. I was going to see Tom, unnanounced. I knew about those first Friday lunch dates of theirs and I wanted to counteract her spell as soon as possible. There was no answer to my knock but lights were on so I turned the knob and found the door unlocked. I walked in. I'd never seen a dead person before so I got sick and scared. I didn't know what to think. I shut the door, left, and just wanted to forget the whole thing. I didn't think I'd learned anything important that night so I kept my mouth shut. However, now that this 'Aton-Smith' is dead and, from your appearance here, not the murderer, it seems that I did see something. I didn't recognize the person at the time, but we've since been 'team mates.' As I was driving to Tom's, I saw someone else driving past me on the same block. One of your friends."

I've heard some hearing people say that they know the truth when they hear it. I assume there's more boast than truth to a statement like that, but I'd just known the truth when I'd seen it. I won't make any claims at being invincible. If California taught me anything, it was humility. In that particular instance, with that particular person, however, I knew. To the bottom of my soul I knew. When I like people I'm more prone to believe what they say. I didn't like Charlotte and was prepared to doubt her, but I saw what I saw. It was in her hands, in her face, in her eyes. She was not sad that Sarah was dead, but she hadn't killed her. Whether she had lip read Tom calling out Sarah's name was irrelevant.

"Who?" I asked.

She told me.

18

Upon receiving Charlotte's revelation everything became clear to me. The who, of course, and also the why. And, unfortunately, my own stupidity. I need never have visited the University of the Sun, much less enrolled. The answer had been given to me, from the horse's mouth long before that misadventure and I had missed it.

Not missed it really. I'd understood the words clearly but not the meaning, not the referents. Communication and language are not synonymous. A slap in the face is not language but usually clear communication. English, American Sign Language, Swahili, etc. can be used to inform or enlighten or to trick or mislead.

In my situation the issue was even deeper than that. There had been no intentional deception from the murderer to me at the critical moment. The killer had not been in control of his/her communication. (Sorry to have to use an awkward construction like "his/her" but since I don't want to reveal who just yet, English leaves me no choice. In signing it's easy to avoid the inclusive male pronoun. English should adopt a neutral pronoun like "te" or "heshe.")

Especially frustrating was that I'd have caught the murderer's true meaning if I'd only paid closer attention to the meaning of the non-verbal clues. We deaf people are supposed to be better at that, and we are. I'd just blown it. Maybe California was addling my brain. Just in case I failed again I wrote a note explaining what I knew, (I always have paper and pencil in my car in case of emergency), stopped at the Fremont post

123

office, bought a stamped envelope, and sent the letter to Russel Jefferson.

From Fremont I drove to San Francisco. Since I'd been spending so much time in Berkeley and the East Bay I decided to cross the water via the Hayward-San Mateo Bridge. It was always less crowded than the Bay Bridge anyway. My route to the city took me past the San Francisco Airport, South San Francisco, and Candlestick Park, home of the S.F. Giants. I could write reams about the nuttiness about playing baseball there, but that would be an irrelevant digression. The case had nothing to do with baseball, nor books, nor even money. I had been right in the first place. The bottom line was a three letter word beginning with S and ending with X. You have to figure out the middle letter all by yourself.

I reached Bay St., parked, and had to remember to curb my wheels. I wanted my car to still be there when I was finished. Now that it was day time and I was wide awake I was impressed with the location of Rudy's place. He was near the top of the street/hill so his top floor bay window would give him a beautiful view of Alcatraz and the bay—when there wasn't fog. He told me he'd been lucky. A friend of a friend had been moving out. He'd just been in the right place at the right time.

I pressed his buzzer, put my hand on the door knob, turned it, and pressed inward. After a few seconds the door gave way. I couldn't hear him buzz me but I've learned how those security systems work. His elevator was creaky and slow but with my cast it was preferable to the stairs. He opened his apartment door shortly after I knocked.

"Hi Rudy."

"Hi Bob, this is a surprise."

"I know. I would have called, through Nancy, but I wanted to see you alone. I have a problem that I have to talk about."

"I thought you were the counselor."

"I am but often we need help ourselves and this is a particularly sticky situation. I've never handled anything quite like it before. Can I come in?"

124

"Sure, but I don't know if I can help."

I looked around the living room more carefully this time and admired how tastefully it was furnished. There was a sophisticated looking stereo system, an old roll-top desk, a rocking chair, a redwood coffee table, and the convertable sofa I'd slept on before. The view of the bay dominated the room when the sun was out, like it was then.

I chose the rocking chair and Rudy took a seat on the sofa. His shoulder was still bandaged but he looked in far less pain than when we'd escaped together from the hospital.

"So," he said, "what's up? Aren't you and Nancy getting along?"

"Well," I said, "That is a problem, but that's not what I came to talk about."

"What then?"

"I know."

"What do you mean, 'you know'?"

"About Sarah's murder, who did it, how, and why. I'm missing some details, but they're unimportant. My problem is that I don't know what to do with my information."

"I don't understand."

"Good counseling technique. You're forcing me to make my meaning clear. I do that with my students often." He said nothing. "Well," I continued, "here goes. You didn't mean to kill her, did you?"

"What?"

"You loved her, and she decided, after all this time, to go back to Tom, didn't she? You followed her but you only wanted to talk her out of it. That's just the outline, but I'm right, aren't I?"

He stayed silent.

"My problem now, is what to do. I can't let Tom go to prison for life for a murder he didn't commit but I honestly like you. And I owe you my life. Do I owe you yours in return? If so, what about Tom? Do you see my problem now?"

He stayed silent.

"That's my ethical dilemma, but this whole mess is even more complicated. I know what I know but I don't have much evidence. I have a witness who can place you near the scene of the crime at the right time, but not much more. It wouldn't be enough to convict you, that's for sure.

"I've told Tom's lawyer and he can use my 'theory' as an alternate explanation. It might be enough to have the jury find reasonable doubt, but it might not. It would certainly cause people to be suspicious about you, however, and damage their faith in the heliotherapy center."

He stayed silent.

"Well, what do I do? And what will you do. It's a short flight or a ten hour drive to Mexico. If I had a note from you, exonerating Tom, I'd feel in no hurry to deliver it. I don't need to know where you're going so I couldn't tell even if I were asked."

"Aren't you worried," he said, "sitting all alone here with a murderer?"

"No. You didn't kill her in cold blood and you couldn't kill me. You're not that kind of man. You could cover your tracks efficiently, after the fact, but you neither love nor hate me. I'm safe.

"When you killed Sarah you weren't in control of yourself. I saw the demon in your soul written on your face that evening in the jaccuzi after racquetball. You told me about hating Tom for having a hold on Sarah, but I misunderstood the 'him' you were talking about. I thought you meant Aton."

"I see," he said.

"There is one detail I'd like to check on. The other book-end, where is it?"

"The bottom of the bay."

"That's what I thought." At least I'd made one correct assumption.

"So," I continued, "back to the basic question, the reason I came. Can you help me?"

"We went out to dinner that night and she told me. She tried to soften it by saying I hadn't done anything wrong, but she dumped me. She was going to marry him. After loving me she was going to marry him. I couldn't believe it. I tried to tell her she couldn't leave me but she just got stubborn.

"She walked out of the restaurant on me. I followed her to Tom's but she was even more stubborn there. The more she refused to listen the madder I got. I don't know why I picked up that bookend. I don't even remember it clearly. Maybe I don't want to. She shouldn't have let me in to continue the argument. She shouldn't have opened the door."

I'm not a feminist but also don't consider myself a chauvinist, though there are probably people who would, depending on their views, stick me with one label or the other. I believe there's nothing wrong with a grown many crying. (I have, once, right after I got Ellen's letter, and I'm not ashamed of it.)

Rudy's tears, however, were a sorry sight. I watched the total collapse of a man. Strength and winning, that's all his life had ever been, a compensation for the loveless upbringing. His outward cool, the rational intellect, they were all part of an elaborate cover for a frightened, desperately unhappy, self-hating man. Heliotherapy hadn't cured him after all.

At that moment I could have done anything with him. His whole self had fallen apart. It would take years of therapy to rebuild it. At that moment I could have brought him to the police station, led him to the roof and walked him off, gotten myself named his heir. You name it, he was my man.

Such power and control is frightening especially because all those thoughts ran through my mind. I don't ever want to be in a position like that again. It's a responsibility that's too heavy to bear.

What I did was none of the above. I got him to sign a confession. I told him I'd wait a day before I brought it to the police. When I left, he was still crying.

19

Nancy wasn't home when I got there. I went straight to bed. I hurt everywhere. The walking cast was heavy and painful. My ribs were sore and my head ached.

Mentally, I was only a little better. You'd think that I'd have been elated, but I wasn't. I had done what I came for, solved the mystery, and Tom would soon be out of jail. But I wasn't elated, just tired.

My "success" had come with unpleasant and unexpected attendant consequences. A stranger had been hurt and a new friend destroyed in his own eyes. I'd made an important decision that was very questionable. I'd given a murderer a chance to escape scot-free. An unintentional murder who had saved my life, but a killer nonetheless. The mess created by the murder seemed never ending. My ego and self-image had been taken down a peg or two. Never again would I investigate a murder. Never. Like E.T., I felt out of place. All I wanted to do was go home.

As false as it would be, I knew I'd be received at home as a hero. News of my exploits would reach the East before I did. My failures, mistakes, and shitty behavior would not be reported. Even if I tried to spread the truth it would be discounted. All that would matter would be that I had saved Tom. In the eyes of my friends I'd be a hero, but not in mine. As unsettling as the undeserved adulation would be, I still wanted to go home. I couldn't take any more of the California sun.

Nancy came in later, joined me in bed, and once again, my love making was perfunctory. This time she got up and turned on the lights so we could talk easily. She asked me what was wrong and I gave her the news. As I was fully aware, to her it was all bad. Her boss and friend was a murderer and I was leaving.

"You've been wonderful to me," I said, "but I've got to get out of California."

"I'm sure you could find a job here. You could stay with me, rent free, as long as you like."

"It's not my job, though it's a good one and I like it. It's certainly not you. There's a lot I have to think about, internal things, and I can't do it here in California. I never intended to be a private investigator. I don't see how anyone could stand doing it for a living. I'll write, I promise. I'll be okay after a while, I know I will. Then you can come visit me. I'll show off the nation's capital, show you my hospitality. Would you like that?"

"Of course, silly man."

"Thanks for understanding. I need that now."

"I just don't want to lose you."

I hugged her, she hugged me, and we loved again, this time with our old fire and fun. I'd probably get fired if I suggested to a student that the answer to depression and doubt lay in good sex, but that was what I was feeling. Nancy's help that night might have been short lived, but at the time it was very necessary.

Despite the good loving, it was not a pleasant good-bye (Are they ever?) the next morning. I wanted to wind up the business with Tom without her. She understood that but didn't want me to leave at all. She made one more plea for me to stay, or at least go just to wrap up business and come back. I had to say no again.

"Is there someone else in Washington?" she asked.

"No."

"Really?"

"Honest, there isn't." I wasn't lying and she knew it but the 'someone else' fear is so often there in break-ups where there isn't anyone else. And it's not that irrational a fear since

130

only the tense is wrong. When things go wrong when there *is* no other, sooner or later there *will be* one.

"At least love me one last time" she said.

I replied in the affirmative without words.

She made one last attempt to keep me, also without words. It was a wonderful attempt, one I'll always remember. It's ironic, as good as Nancy was to me, if the problem had been another woman, Nancy would have won the war. But the enemy was too vague and unsubstantial to be fought.

As it was, when I left, she was crying.

I walked into Jefferson's office feeling bad about Nancy but resolved about what I had to do. He was with another client so I had to wait fifteen minutes. I asked him if he had gotten my letter. He hadn't so I handed him Rudy's confession. "Here's everything we need," I said.

He read it carefully. "You're right," he said, "this should be sufficient. It should be shown to the police immediately."

"Fine. Who should do it? You or me?"

"I think I should. I'm Mr. Hayes' lawyer and I can start the procedures for his immediate release."

"Great. I'll go to the jail now and deliver the good news."

"If everything goes smoothly I should be able to meet you within the hour."

"Fantastic. This whole thing finally seems over. Let me run to tell the only person who'll be more happy to hear that than me."

"You mean," Tom said, "that she was in my place, waiting for me, to tell me that she wanted to marry me, and that's why she was killed?"

Apparently, Tom still needed my help, this time in my more familiar role as a counselor. I'd told him what had happened and he'd heard me correctly, but what an interpretation he was putting on the facts.

My mother would have said that, like the woman in "Looking for Mr. Goodbar," Sarah was killed because she was screwing around. (My mother needs a course in consciousness raising.) Another analyst might comment that Sarah was killed because she went to Tom's house too early; if she waited till Tom got home she'd still be alive. Though there's a kernel of truth in all of the above, they're all, in my opinion, approaching the situation backwards.

What Tom was really saying was "She was killed because of me."

"No, no, no," I told him, (even though he'd said a truth) "don't say she was killed because . . . Remember your English grammar. It's better to use the active voice than the passive. Rudy killed her. She wasn't killed because . . . Rudy killed her because he couldn't stand the thought of losing her . . . He didn't like losing at anything. Then, for the first time in his adult life, he falls in love—and he lost her. Remember what happened to me when Ellen broke our engagement?"

"Of course."

"As bad as that was for me it must have been nothing compared to the turmoil, rage, and despair inside Rudy."

As soon as I said that I had a vague feeling of unease, a premonition that the case might not be over after all, that I might have made one final mistake.

Tom must have read my mind. "What's wrong?" he asked.

"Nothing, I hope. It's not connected to your release, so back to my point. Do you see what I mean? You were *not, not, not,* responsible for her murder."

"But . . ."

"No buts, you weren't. Period."

"Well . . ."

I could see I'd have a long struggle with this stubborn friend of mine, but I'd do it long distance, via the mail. From the jail I was intending to hop into a cab to the airport, and take the first flight home.

Our conversation was interrupted by the entrance of Jefferson and Sergeant Grimsley. "Mr. Hayes," she said, "you're free to go. We regret our mistake and hope you understand."

132

Tom, now free to act, came over to my table and hugged me. Men don't hug each other often enough. If it hadn't been for his hug, in fact, I don't know if I could have stood what I was to learn soon after that. "Buddy," he said, "I don't just owe you one. I owe you anything. Whatever you want, it's yours."

"How about five bucks for cab fare to the airport and another five for a big burrito when I get there?"

"It will take another few minutes to get your personal effects," Jefferson said to Tom. He took a ten from his wallet and gave it to Tom. "I'll add this to my bill."

I got the ten and Tom went to change and pack. He wanted me to wait so I could see him out of jail, a free man, before I left. I agreed.

Jefferson, the sergeant, and I walked outside to wait for Tom. It was there that they hit me with the other news.

"You'll be happy to hear," the sergeant said, "that the driver of the other car in your accident is off the critical list. He is expected to recover fully."

"Thank you," I said. "That is good to hear. It takes a load off my conscience."

"There is, however," she continued, "news that's not so good. Rudolph Alexis' body was found this morning in the waters by the Golden Gate. Several motorists saw him jump from the bridge shortly after dawn."

They were only words but they came like a blow to my already concussed head. Rudy had saved my life and I hadn't saved his. I could have walked him to the police station the night before. He'd be in jail, but he'd be alive.

Me and my stupidity. I'm supposed to be a counselor. No more classic case for suicide risk could be presented than the condition I'd seen Rudy in. And I had thought he'd take my suggestion and go to Mexico. Stupid, stupid, stupid. I tried to excuse myself by saying I'd been too tired and too preoccupied to think straight, but I wasn't buying it. I had been in a position of responsibility. I hadn't wanted it, but I'd had no choice but to make a choice. And I'd made the worst one.

I'm not sure what I would have done if Tom had not come charging out of the door to the jail at that moment. He saw my face, got the news from Jefferson and Grimsley, and became my savior. I did ride in a cab to the airport and I did get on the next plane to Washington but only because Tom rode to the airport with me and led me around like a sheep. He even called Washington so that other friends were waiting for me on my arrival.

Six months later Tom left California, moved to D.C., and found a job working in an elementary school. By that time I had recovered. Work had helped and so had time, but the most important single factor had been a card from California. It arrived two weeks after I did. It was from Tom and Nancy. It was a thank you gift that they had collaborated on—a certificate giving me an unlimited charge account at Cody's bookstore for one year.

It made me laugh and made me cry. I cried because of the realization of the kind of friends I had. A present to match my wildest dreams. I laughed because I had to go back to Berkeley (and Nancy) to collect it.

Ritual Disclaimer

To the best of my knowledge, there is not, nor ever has been, a University of the Sun or a Heliotherapy Center of California, but that surprises me.

Postscript: On Sign Language, Lip Reading, English, and Communication

Since this book is narrated by Bob, a deaf man, it was impossible for me, a hearing man, to include the awe I feel when watching people like Bob communicate. Because of the different modes used by American Sign Language (ASL) and English, they can and do interact in more complex ways than two spoken languages. There is no Bob Brewer but there are deaf people who have all his communication skills.

People like him have the ability to express themselves in English, ASL, or in a combination of the two. They can pick their words and signs depending on which language explains a concept clearer, faster, or, in that particular situation, is more fun. They can make jokes and puns in either language or on how the languages overlap. (Picture a car pool using the most common definition of pool.)

I could also not include in the novel how beautiful sign language can be. I wish my readers could have seen one of my unpaid editors describe my car chase scene down Lombard Street—via signs. It was more descriptive and more graceful than I could ever do in words. And that's just one example.

For those people interested in classes in sign language I suggest contacting your local state school for the deaf or write to the National Association of the Deaf, 814 Thayer Ave. Silver Spring, Md. 20910. For books on sign language; dictionaries, grammar texts, linguistic research, etc. write or visit the Gallaudet College Bookstore, Washington, D.C. 20002.

I need to make some comments on lip reading. I expect some readers to criticise the book by saying that Bob lip reads too well. There is some truth to that criticism. According to text books, no person, hearing or deaf, could lip read as well as he does. For the vast majority of people, the text books are right. There are, however, a few deaf individuals who can do everything I describe Bob doing. It's hard to believe, but I've seen them in action. Trust me.

Bob's command of English is also extraordinary. It is extremely difficult to learn a spoken language when you can't hear. Hearing children usually learn to *read* English when they go to school but they already know, on the average, over 2 thousand words and the basic structure and grammar. They aren't taught it, they just pick it up, through their ears, via play, conversation, T.V. etc. Despite the difficulty, there are over 30 profoundly, congenitally deaf individuals with Ph.D. degrees.

There is enough information about deafness and deaf people to fill an entire room of the Gallaudet College Library. If you're interested and in the Washington, D.C. area, its worth a visit. If not you can write to them.

For more information on crime and crime detection, you're on your own.